"The Third Condition Is That You Marry Me."

Connor's tone was smooth and businesslike. He caught her gaze and held it.

Laurel stood in shock, staring back at him.

"Marry you? Are you mad?"

"I've never felt saner in my life." Connor took a step toward her, and Laurel actually felt her knees shake.

"Why?" she demanded. "Why in heaven's name do you want to marry me? The whole idea is just...insane, Connor."

He shrugged his broad shoulders; his sensuous mouth lifted in a small, private smile. "Because I know now I should have married you seven years ago."

"That's ridiculous," she countered.

"Oh, I don't know about that, Laurel," Connor stated, smiling. "If I ever had any doubt, that kiss just convinced me otherwise."

Dear Reader,

Silhouette is celebrating its 20th anniversary throughout 2000! So, to usher in the first summer of the millennium, why not indulge yourself with six powerful, passionate, provocative love stories from Silhouette Desire?

Jackie Merritt returns to Desire with a MAN OF THE MONTH who's *Tough To Tame.* Enjoy the sparks that fly between a rugged ranch manager and the feisty lady who turns his world upside down! Another wonderful romance from RITA Award winner Caroline Cross is in store for you this month with *The Rancher and the Nanny,* in which a rags-to-riches hero learns trust and love from the riches-to-rags woman who cares for his secret child.

Watch for Meagan McKinney's *The Cowboy Meets His Match*—an octogenarian matchmaker sets up an ice-princess heiress with a virile rodeo star. The Desire theme promotion THE BABY BANK, about sperm-bank client heroines who find love unexpectedly, concludes with Susan Crosby's *The Baby Gift.* Wonderful newcomer Sheri WhiteFeather offers another irresistible Native American hero with *Cheyenne Dad.* And Kate Little's hero reunites with his lost love in a marriage of convenience to save her from financial ruin in *The Determined Groom.*

So come join in the celebration and start your summer off on the supersensual side—by reading all six of these tantalizing Desire books!

Enjoy!

Joan Marlow Golan

Joan Marlow Golan
Senior Editor, Silhouette Desire

Please address questions and book requests to:
Silhouette Reader Service
U.S.: 3010 Walden Ave., P.O. Box 1325, Buffalo, NY 14269
Canadian: P.O. Box 609, Fort Erie, Ont. L2A 5X3

The Determined Groom

Groom

KATE LITTLE

Silhouette® *Desire*

Published by Silhouette Books

America's Publisher of Contemporary Romance

SILHOUETTE BOOKS

ISBN 0-373-76302-6

THE DETERMINED GROOM

Printed in U.S.A.

Books by Kate Little

Silhouette Desire

Jingle Bell Baby #1043
Husband for Keeps #1276
The Determined Groom #1302

KATE LITTLE

claims to have lots of experience with romance—"the *fictional* kind, that is," she is quick to clarify. She has been both an author and an editor of romance fiction for over fifteen years. She believes that a good romance will make the reader experience all the tension, thrills and agony of falling madly, deeply and wildly in love. She enjoys watching the characters in her books go crazy for each other, but hates to see the blissful couple disappear when it's time for them to live happily ever after. In addition to writing romance novels, Kate also writes fiction and nonfiction for young adults. She lives on Long Island, New York, with her husband and daughter.

One

He couldn't say why he had returned.

A premonition perhaps. A need to touch home base before flying on to greater heights, a new job and a new life in New York City. His first position out of college, the first step in a career that looked bright and full of possibilities. He was due to start on Monday morning, his graduate degree in business in hand, the ink barely dry. He'd already moved his few possessions into a new apartment in Chelsea that he would share with a friend. Everything was set. But for some strange reason, Connor had felt the need to set foot on the Cape for a few days. To breathe the salty ocean-fresh air all day, and at night, linger on the porch of the old cottage that had barely changed since his boyhood.

Since his mother's death years ago, his father had kept everything in their small home the same. Connor often wished his mother had lived to see his graduation. She would have been so proud. Unlike his father, she had believed he could do anything with his life that he wanted to.

Once she was gone, Connor had not come home very often. He and his father didn't get along. Never had. Few questions were asked about Connor's absence, no excuses necessary. There was nothing left for him here anymore, Connor thought as he drove along the winding road that led to the entrance of the Sutherland estate. Nothing but memories.

He didn't really know why he'd come home for the weekend. Or why he had accepted Charles Sutherland's impromptu invitation to attend the party at the main house that night. Perhaps he'd accepted simply out of a feeling of obligation to Charles, who had been so generous to him in so many ways. That debt could never truly be repaid.

The imposing sight of the Sutherland mansion at the end of the long curved driveway cut into his reverie and captured his full attention. The house was lit up like Grand Central Station, the portico bustling with guests as valets helped them emerge from shining luxury cars and long black limousines. He'd parked his own car at the end of the driveway, just in case the party became too tedious and he resorted to a quick getaway.

But the moment he spotted Laurel Sutherland, he knew with utter certainty why he had come home.

The instant her turquoise gaze met his—her expression, first shocked, then so very pleased—he understood. Her warm easy smile went right to his heart, like an arrow flying straight and true, striking its mark with bittersweet precision.

She was surrounded by her guests, friends and family, the men in white dinner jackets, the women glittering with jewels and silken finery. Lauren herself, a vision in a summer gown of some filmy azure blue fabric, her tanned smooth shoulders bare, her skin flawless, her long golden hair pulled to one side with a jeweled clip, the rest floating over her shoulders as she moved across the softly lit patio to greet him.

In her graceful form and the delicate lines of her face he saw a glimmer of the girl he had known so long ago. The brave comrade who had raced beside him on sunny beaches and through the dark, cool woods all summer long. His playmate, his friend, his kindred spirit.

And yet, she was a woman now. A beautiful young woman in all her glory.

The promise of her girlhood features fulfilled in a most exquisite way, he thought. Transformed from sweet innocence to alluring mystery, the high cheekbones, full lips and straight, delicate nose as perfectly formed as any famous face on the cover of a magazine. Yet, Laurel's face glowed with something more, Connor thought. Her radiant spirit—the daring, stubborn streak of that spunky tomboy shining through, like a light from within.

She held out her hand to him, the look in her eyes bright, excited and also relieved. As if, all this time, she had been waiting for him. Worried he wouldn't arrive. But now he had come.

And she felt contented. Completed.

As he too felt, moving toward her.

In a blinding bolt, the realization struck. This is why he had come. For Laurel. Of course. It seemed suddenly so obvious now. So right.

* * *

As his large hand enfolded hers, he felt the soft skin, the delicate bones. He bent to kiss her cheek and inhaled the flowery scent of her hair. He drew away and gazed down at her to find a tender smile on her lips and a knowing look in her eyes that caused his heart to shudder with awareness. He did not release her hand, nor did she make any move to break contact.

"My father told me he met you in town. He said you might come," she said. "But I wasn't sure you would. I remembered how much you hated fancy parties."

Her voice sounded different, deeper, richer, and the music of it worked a special magic on him.

"Still hate parties," he replied, flashing a grin. "But I wanted to see you."

Maybe seeing Laurel hadn't been Connor's conscious reason for coming. But as he said the words aloud, he knew it was true.

When he'd met Charles Sutherland in town that day, he'd asked about Laurel, tried to picture how she'd turned out since he'd last seen her. How long had it been? Five years, since her mother had died when she was sixteen. He had attended the funeral, offered his comfort and condolences as best as he could, but had barely spoken to her after that day.

After Madeleine Sutherland's death, there were no more summers on the Cape for Laurel and her family. His father said that Charles Sutherland found it too painful to return to the place that held so many memories for him. Connor could understand, but regretted the way Charles's grief kept Laurel away. After that time, Laurel and her older brother, Phillip, attended boarding schools during the fall and winter and spent their summers abroad, on organized trips for wealthy teenagers. Yes, they'd lost touch completely after Mrs. Sutherland had died.

Charles had spoken proudly of his daughter's accomplishments, how well she'd done at the Ivy League college she'd attended, her acceptance to a prestigious law school. Adding, almost as an afterthought, the news that she'd soon be married. A very nice boy she'd met in college, Charles explained. The wedding was less than a month away, in fact. Charles was hosting a party for the happy couple that very night.

"Won't you drop by, Connor?" Charles had urged him. "I know Laurel would love to see you."

Connor had agreed to come. He owed Charles Sutherland so much. All the opportunity and advantages in his life that now granted him such a promising future. A debt he'd vowed to someday repay. Of course he'd come to the party. It was generous, as always, of Charles to invite him. To treat Connor as a friend of the family, an equal, when in fact they both knew that Connor was no more than the caretaker's son.

As he returned to his father's modest cottage and prepared to visit the Sutherland estate, Connor refused to acknowledge the way his heart had clenched when Laurel's father had told him about her engagement. But he could not push away the many images of Laurel that had drifted through his mind all day— memories of the adventures they'd shared, their squabbles and reconciliations, the secrets they had entrusted to each other. He was eager to see her. And curious to meet the man she had decided to marry.

His thoughts and feelings about her all day gave no hint to the impact he now felt, standing beside her. The flood of emotions was staggering, like a giant wave crashing down over him. It took all his self-control to keep up a polite front.

All he knew now was that he did not want to let go of her hand. Not soon. Not ever. If anything, he wanted to pull her closer, draw her slender form to his side and bury his face in her silky hair.

Could she guess? Was she feeling anything like this for him?

When he met her gaze, she appeared to have been studying him. Connor wasn't vain about his looks, but he knew by now that women found him attractive—and told him so. They liked his thick dark hair and deep brown eyes, the cleft in his strong chin and the flash of his even white teeth when he smiled. Connor never gave much thought to his looks, but as Laurel's appraising gaze swept over him, he hoped that she liked what she saw.

With a slight, sly smile on her lips, she craned her head back and stared up to take in his entire six foot two inches.

"My word, you got tall," she observed lightly. "Remember how you worried that you wouldn't?"

He laughed. It seemed a hundred years ago that he'd wasted so much time worrying needlessly about that boyhood concern. He'd forgotten he'd confided that fear to anyone. But he must have told Laurel.

"You turned out pretty well yourself," he observed, his gaze sweeping down to take in every lovely inch of her.

She was tall. But not too tall. Just right, he thought. Long arms and legs, like a model. But without that starved-greyhound look he hated. She still looked as if she worked out, but now she had curves in all the right places.

"Well, thanks. How nice of you to notice." The corner of her mouth twisted up in a playful grin Connor found amazingly sexy and appealing. "Is that the line you use on the girls in New York?"

"I don't date very much," he answered with a laugh. "Maybe I should work on my technique." It was the truth, too. For the past six years he'd been too busy keeping up his grades and working at the part-time jobs that supplemented his scholarships.

"Maybe," she replied quietly. She paused, looked out at the crowd then back at him, her expression dreamy, wistful. "It's good to see you again, Connor," she added softly.

"It's great to see you," he said, his voice thick with emotion.

A jazz ensemble at the far end of the patio started to play a torchy ballad Connor had always liked, but at that moment, the familiar song seemed to take on a special meaning.

"Dance with me?"

She smiled her assent and he led her out to the dance floor, then took her in his arms. She willingly moved closer to him, her long smooth arms looped around his neck, her head turned to the side so that her cheek nearly brushed his shoulder. He took a deep breath, inhaled her perfume and the special, unique scent of her warm skin. He felt intoxicated, drugged, cast under a powerful spell. As he tilted his head to look down at her, it was with willful effort that he suppressed an urge to dip his head just a few inches lower to drop a soft kiss on her full, berry-red mouth.

How wonderful that would feel, he thought as she swayed seductively against him. How amazingly wonderful.

But once he got started, how would he stop? It was hard enough to control himself, holding her like this. Her slender body fit perfectly next to his own, he thought. His bare palm made contact with the silky skin on her back, exposed by the low back-line of her gown, and Connor felt his heartbeat race. He had the immediate urge to run his hand up and down her bare back, to caress and explore every inch of smooth skin. To slide his hands down the curve of her hip and cup her adorable bottom.

In short, to create a scandalizing scene, right here on the patio of the Sutherland summer mansion. A scene that would be talked about in certain circles for years to come.

Laurel asked him questions, eager to catch up on the years since they'd been apart. She listened with genuine interest as he told her about his college years, his studies and the many part-time jobs he'd worked to get through school. He told her all about the new apartment in New York and his new job. He asked her questions, too, carefully sidestepping the subject of her upcoming marriage. Yet, all the while they spoke, his pulse pounded furiously, a distant part of his mind was spinning out of control with rapturous images and emotions.

Had he ever danced with Laurel before? Really danced, not just playing around with music on the radio? He could only remember one time, at a Labor Day barbecue; she was sixteen and he was twenty. They were both at an awkward stage, Connor reflected, if Laurel had ever gone through such a phase.

She had the requisite braces and unruly hair, the gawky angles to her figure and a touching shyness. Some stuck-up prep-school boy she had a crush on had treated her heartlessly all night long. He'd even gone so far as to tease her when she asked him to dance. Connor had watched as the tears welled up in her eyes, and did the only thing he could do—short of socking the other kid in the nose—tug Laurel out on the dance floor himself. He wasn't much of a dancer at the time and had looked and felt ridiculous. But seeing Laurel's tears turn to laughter had been worth it.

That night he had kissed her, hadn't he? Connor had all but forgotten that moment, until now. A soft, fleeting kiss squarely on her lips, which had brought the color rushing up to her cheeks, and left her wide-eyed and stunned. The kiss had been half-friendly...half something else. But it had ended right there, with Connor realizing that, no matter what was simmering between them, Laurel was far too young for them to be romantically involved.

It wasn't much different this time, was it? Connor reflected. Laurel was a beautiful, elegant, charming woman and, holding her in his arms, he felt the envy of every man in the place. Inexplicable feelings still simmered between them. And he still yearned to kiss her. Not an innocent peck either, but a kiss that would lead to much more.

And Laurel was still out of reach. Off limits. Tonight, even more than before.

How had that happened? And how had he lived all this time without her?

The unbidden thought flashed through his mind. Connor considered it, feeling at first totally crazy and then utterly sane. Saner and more content than he had in a long time.

As he continued to make polite small talk, another part of his mind repeated the same refrain: *This is Laurel. My Laurel. We're together again.*

Holding her in his arms, looking into her eyes, every loose end in his life had suddenly fallen into place.

Then their conversation stopped and they slowly moved closer, their bodies moving in rhythm to the music as if one. Did she feel it too? he wondered. He believed that she must be feeling some-thing…extraordinary, as he did. He simply could not be experiencing this amazing revelation alone.

"Connor." She said his name slowly, as if savor-ing the sound as it rolled off her tongue. "I've thought about you a lot these past years, wondered how you were doing…" Her voice trailed off. "I missed you," she confessed. She looked up at him, with clear blue eyes that conveyed so much more than words could ever say.

Her simple admission went right through him, touched his heart, his very soul, ringing within, loud and true. And he knew he was right. She felt it, too.

"I've thought about you too, Laurel," he replied. He tilted his head back and looked down at her. "I've missed you, too. Very much."

He watched as the impact of his words registered in her expression. She looked surprised at first, then happy, and finally, her gaze was sweet and tender. She turned away, a slight smile on her lips, and he tucked her close again. She had always been so open and honest with her emotions. So trusting. He could never hurt her. He could never betray that trust.

I have missed you, Laurel, he added silently. But until tonight, I didn't know how much. Something in my life making me feel restless, driven, unsatisfied. Some elusive need, pushing me on. Wanting to achieve, to excel. To measure up in someone's eyes. Not for my family. Not even for myself. For someone. Who? For you, Laurel. It was all for you. And of all the women I've met, one or two came close to feeling right, and yet, still fell short. That was it, of course, all those years. I'd been comparing them to you.

And never even realized it.

Connor felt the music wash over him, cherishing the feeling of Laurel in his arms. The singer's soulful voice did full justice to the song's romantic lyrics, describing the magical moment when love is first discovered, first realized. Suddenly Connor wanted to laugh out loud at his own foolishness, his own blindness. He felt lighthearted. Released of some crushing burden he wasn't even aware he'd been carrying. But now he knew. And the entire world looked different to him, bright, fresh, new, as if washed clean by a summer storm.

On impulse, he lifted her hand to his lips and kissed her fingertips. He saw her eyes flutter shut for a moment and heard her sigh. The sound, no louder than a breath, drove him wild. He imagined sweeping her up in his arms and carrying her down to the beach, making love to her all night long just to elicit more of those soft seductive sighs. He gently squeezed her hand and then felt something cold and sharp bite into his skin. He knew without looking. Her engagement ring. Of course. The classic, square-cut diamond— large enough to impress but one that could never be called ostentatious.

Then, as if magically summoned by Connor's thoughts, the fiancé appeared, emerging from the crowd to stand beside them on the dance floor. Connor recognized him instantly from the peeved expression on his smooth face.

"Enjoying yourself, sweetheart?" he asked Laurel. He brushed her hair off her shoulder in a gesture that seemed to Connor both blatantly intimate and somehow, mildly disapproving.

"Todd." Laurel's voice sounded husky and slow, as if she had just been rudely awakened from a pleasant dream, Connor thought. Or was that simply his own feeling? Laurel stopped dancing and Connor had no choice but to release her.

"This is my old friend, Connor Northrup," Laurel said, starting the introductions. "You must have heard me talk about Connor. We go way back."

"Of course. Good old Connor. Boy hero, a friend to all. I remember," Todd assured both of them.

Connor knew that if Todd recalled anything about his relationship with Laurel it would most likely be that Connor was the son of the family servants, the caretaker—and sometimes chauffeur—and the housekeeper. From the cool, condescending way Todd looked him over and the curt nod of greeting, Connor felt certain that this was the case.

"Connor, this is my fiancé, Todd Parson."

"Congratulations on your engagement," Connor offered politely. "You're a lucky man."

"Thanks, Connor." Todd slipped his arm around Laurel's waist and pulled her toward him. "Guess I chased her until she caught me," he joked.

Connor laughed politely along with Laurel, but he could see how Todd's little joke had stung her. He

didn't like Todd Parson. He supposed that most
women would find the guy good-looking, but Connor
didn't like the man's small dark eyes, his slicked-back
hair, his cocky attitude. His entire demeanor screamed
of the right family name, the right schools and connections. But Connor felt, deep in the marrow of his
very bones, that this arrogant young man, who came
equipped with all the advantages of wealth and class,
was not nearly good enough for Laurel.

"Stan and Louise just arrived. They've been asking
for you," Todd mentioned privately to Laurel. "I really think you ought to say hello to them. Especially
since Stan sent me that new client last week."

"Oh, yes. I guess I'd better," Laurel agreed, scan-
ning the crowd. Then she glanced up at Connor, her
turquoise eyes shimmering with some private message for him alone. Clearly, she seemed sorry to leave
him. But there was something more. What was it exactly? Connor wondered as he tried to understand.
Telegraphing her reluctance to leave him? Her sense
of being torn suddenly between her promise to Todd
and the feelings ignited by their reunion?

"I'll see you later, Connor. We'll catch up some
more, okay?" Laurel said as Todd began to sweep
her back into the crowd.

"Sure thing," Connor replied easily, though he felt
anything but.

Laurel nodded, then turned to respond to some request from Todd that Connor could not hear. Todd's
face looked a bit flushed, as if he'd had too much to
drink or was simply irritated, annoyed at Laurel for
some reason.

Jealous maybe, Connor thought. Had he been in
Todd's place and found his fiancé in the arms of an-

other man with that dreamy expression on her face, he would have felt the same.

Connor watched as the couple disappeared into the laughing, milling crowd and then walked off in search of a drink. His head pounded and a bitter knot twisted in his gut. He was jealous of Todd Parson. Out of his head with jealousy. And what right did he have to feel this way? Absolutely no right at all.

Except that he did. For the profound, amazing feelings for Laurel he'd so newly discovered seemed to grant him the right.

Was he fooling himself? Or had he and Laurel discovered something rare and special here tonight? If so, did they even have time to figure it out before her wedding day?

How ironic, Connor thought as he lifted a glass of champagne off a passing silver platter. He'd known Laurel most of his life. And now, when perhaps he was just coming to realize what she meant to him— what she *could* mean to him—it was too late. She was claimed by another man.

Connor knew full well that he should respect Laurel's commitment. In all his life, even as a boy, he'd lived by a strong moral and ethical code and found it hard to imagine himself violating those standards. He certainly didn't think much of men who cheated on their romantic partners, or tried to break up a couple. Especially a couple who planned to be married.

Yet, all these rules and standards didn't seem to apply here. They didn't seem relevant to him and Laurel, not now anyway. All the rules and ethical standards in the world couldn't come close to overshadowing what he felt in his heart. He'd long known the quote, "All's fair in love and war." But until tonight, until the moment he pondered the ethical side of pursuing his newfound feelings for Laurel, he'd never understood it.

For to Connor's mind, when it came to questions of right and wrong, it suddenly didn't seem right that Laurel could marry another man. Just as it didn't seem right that the sun would rise in the west tomorrow and set in the east. Did he dare mention such a thing to her?

Connor shook his dark head as he drained his drink to the bottom of the glass. They needed time. Time to get to know each other again. To test out these amazing, powerful feelings. He'd be asking her to risk everything on a whim, on an impulse.

What if he was wrong?

Slow down, pal, he coached himself. One step at a time. Laurel asked you to hang around so you could talk some more, so that's what you should do.

Connor took a deep breath and set down his empty glass. He gazed around the party and recognized a few faces, friends of Laurel's parents who had often been guests at the estate.

Of course, if they recognized him at all, they would remember him simply as the caretaker's boy. Smart, good-looking, even well-spoken and polite...for a boy from the wrong side of town. How kind of Charles to have taken a liking to the kid. Taken him under his wing. How lucky for the boy to have such a powerful mentor. I understand Charles even helped him get a scholarship to Princeton, they'd whisper. I wonder if he appreciates all that Charles has done for him? they'd add.

And it was all true. Charles Sutherland had helped him a great deal. And while his scholarship had not covered every cost of his education, Connor also believed that working to earn his way in part had also provided an education for him, as valuable as the one he'd received in his classes.

Yes, he had a good deal to thank Charles Sutherland for, Connor reflected again. And how would he repay him? By stepping into his daughter's orderly, well-planned life and creating havoc? By tempting her to be unfaithful to her fiancé, to break her promises and betray her commitments?

Connor searched for Laurel in the crowd and found her. His throat grew tight. The right thing to do was just walk away, right now. Leave for New York tomorrow morning first thing. Couldn't risk seeing her again. Couldn't even risk saying goodbye.

But he didn't think he could do that. Didn't want to do it. She'd be hurt, and he couldn't do that for the world.

Connor stood on the sidelines of the party, sipping another drink and watching the parade of glittering guests. It had been a long time since he'd witnessed such a gathering—perhaps since the last time he'd attended a formal affair at the Sutherlands'. He'd come a long way since those days. Still, he felt awkward and out of place.

He scanned the crowd for a friendly face, hoping to spot his host, Charles Sutherland, whom he had not seen yet. The face he found was familiar yet had never been truly friendly. As Connor's dark gaze locked with the gaze of Laurel's older brother, Phillip, a myriad of emotions and memories flooded through him. Phillip stood in a circle talking, his arm around a beautiful, auburn-haired woman who gazed up at him with rapt attention.

Phillip had been blessed with the same golden-color hair as his sister; thick with a slight wave, it was combed back for a formal look. His eyes were also blue, but a pale, icy shade that suited his cold, calculating nature. Unlike Laurel, his build was stocky and thick. Even as a boy, he'd always been a bit overweight. But as a man, he was able to hide his girth a bit better, especially tonight, under his well-cut attire.

His fair coloring and bronzed complexion—acquired on golf courses, tennis courts and yachts, Connor had no doubt—was set off handsomely by his formal white dinner jacket. All in all, he looked every inch the polished, wealthy young bachelor, heir to the family business his father now ran.

As Connor recollected, Charles had mentioned that Phillip had been working at Sutherland Enterprises since graduating college four years ago. Expecting to take the place over when his father retired, Connor had no doubt. Though everyone who knew both the father and son would know that Phillip would never be half the man Charles Sutherland was.

Phillip nodded in greeting and Connor nodded back, feeling a bitter taste rise in the back of his throat. Then Phillip turned back to his circle and said something that made everyone laugh.

Connor knew instantly that Phillip Sutherland had not changed. He had never met anyone he detested more. Spoiled, manipulative and self-centered, Phillip had done his best to cause trouble for Connor all through their childhood.

Connor could have even tolerated the despicable schemes Phillip carried out to get Connor into trouble, if Phillip had been even the slightest bit kinder to

Laurel. Phillip seemed to have no sense of a loving, protective instinct toward his younger sister. To the contrary, he was either blaming Laurel for his misdeeds or trying to trick her into covering up one of his messes. How many times had Connor, older and not nearly as trusting and naive as Laurel, stepped in, feeling the need to safeguard Laurel from her own brother's machinations? Too many, Connor recollected. He and Phillip had found a lot to fight about. But Connor eventually drew the line at fistfights.

Not that he had ever been afraid of Phillip. Phillip was older, and had been taller and heavier than Connor at the time, but he never got the best of him. It was always Phillip who ran off with a bloody lip or black eye, crying to his father or mother about the rude, crude servant's son. No, Connor had never feared Phillip, but he had learned to fear his own father's wrath, for nothing could make Owen Northrup angrier than hearing that Connor and Phillip had gotten in a scrape.

Owen had disapproved of Connor's friendship with Laurel and would have forbidden Connor to see her at all if he'd had his own way in the matter. Connor thought Owen permitted it only because Charles Sutherland liked Connor so much and seemed to think he was a good influence on his own children.

Owen, however, had stubbornly held on to the belief that no good could come of Connor socializing with what Owen called "his betters." He was also terrified that he and his wife would lose their relatively comfortable and well-paying jobs with the Sutherlands due to one of Connor's fights with Phillip.

To the best of Connor's knowledge, Charles Sutherland had never viewed the boys' scrapes as such a serious problem. In fact, Connor sometimes thought Charles hoped Phillip would glean some valuable lessons from his encounters with Connor.

To avoid facing his father's wrath and the possibility of not being allowed to see Laurel anymore, Connor had often backed off from Phillip's goading challenges. Phillip would gloat, as if Connor lacked courage. For the sake of keeping peace with his father and protecting his relationship with Laurel, Connor had suffered in silence. Though they all knew Connor could whip Phillip with one hand tied behind his back any day of the week. At least, that's what Laurel had always told him.

Connor's reverie was suddenly interrupted by a heavy hand on his shoulder.

"Connor! So glad you could come, son." Connor turned to face Charles's warm and welcoming smile. "Enjoying yourself?"

"Yes, of course. It's quite a party," Connor replied.

"Well, I would have preferred something smaller, at our place in New York. That's where they'll be married. But it was very important to Laurel to come up here, to have a gathering at this house." Charles gazed around, his voice taking a wistful, bittersweet tone, Connor noticed. "She misses her mother, you know. We all miss her."

"She was a wonderful woman," Connor said.

Charles nodded, murmured his thanks and sipped his drink. Connor could see that after all these years it was still very difficult for Charles to speak about his wife. He didn't know what else he might say and felt it best to say nothing more.

Coming here had brought back many memories of

Laurel's mother for him as well. At any moment he expected to see Madeleine Sutherland coming through the French doors from the ballroom, moving gracefully among her guests. Laughing, smiling, looking at her husband in that special way that told the world that Charles Sutherland was the center of her universe. She had been lovely and kind, a gracious woman who always had a special word for him and a way of making him feel welcome in her home. Laurel was turning out to be just like her. No mystery there. Madeleine Sutherland had been devoted to her children and particularly close to Laurel. It was sad that she had not lived to see her daughter's wedding day.

"This was Madeleine's favorite place in the whole world, this house and the gardens and beach. She wanted us to retire here," Charles confided. "I know that's why Laurel wanted the party here tonight. To feel closer to her mother, as if Madeleine had a part in the wedding plans. I've hardly been back since she died." He paused and took a long swallow of his drink. "I don't know. Maybe it was a good thing, opening up the house like this, having this party here. Perhaps it will help us all to put the past to rest somehow," he added, meeting Connor's gaze.

"Yes, a good thing," Connor agreed sympathetically. He could not help but notice the glassy, unshed tears in Charles Sutherland's eyes. He still missed his wife. Missed her with all his heart. That was love, Connor thought. Untouched by time or separation. Even the ultimate separation.

Would he ever know that kind of love for a woman? You could feel that way about Laurel, another voice answered. Maybe you already do.

"Well, enough of this glum and gloomy talk," Charles replied with a forced, bright smile. He patted Connor jovially on the back. "It's time we talked about your future, young man. Tell me more about this job you're starting. Monday, is it?"

"Yes, sir. Monday morning. Bright and early," Connor replied, flattered that Charles remembered about his job when the man obviously had so many more pressing matters on his mind.

"You'll do fine. The organization is lucky to have you," he assured Connor in a fatherly tone. "Oh, and before I forget, there are a few people here I'd like you to meet. Good connections for you down in the city. Now, Ralph Walters over there is an investment banker, a big wheel with Morgan Stanley..."

Connor allowed Charles to lead him into the crowd and was introduced to a few of his host's influential friends. Charles's introductions were always glowing, recounting Connor's achievements and bright prospects to a point that was a breath away from embarrassing. But Connor knew that Charles's enthusiasm was always well meant. In fact, he could not help but feel as if the older man was proudly introducing his own son.

Heaven knew, he'd never had an ounce of such encouragement from his own father. Owen Northrup had always denigrated Connor's ambitions to attend college. More reaching beyond his station in life, was the way Owen saw it. Sure to lead to disappointment and humiliation. As Connor grew older he came to see that his father's criticism, and even suspicion, of his academic achievements was really due to the fact that Owen felt threatened and surpassed by a son who would outgrow his family and make a life for himself far away from the Cape.

After conversing with Charles's Wall Street friends, Connor wandered around the party, waiting for the chance to speak with Laurel again. He caught a glimpse of her now and then, but it never seemed the right moment to approach her.

Finally, the guests began to leave and the crowd thinned. The party was ending. Connor felt self-conscious and could linger no longer. He saw his chance to say goodbye privately to Laurel and swiftly approached her. He felt confused, overwhelmed, his mind whirling with so many possible things he might say to her. Would she meet him tomorrow if he asked?

He approached her as she stood with her back turned. ''Laurel, I just wanted to say good-night....'' His voice trailed off as she spun to face him.

Her beautiful face, her soft smile, the tender light in her eye as she met his gaze overwhelmed him. Connor felt himself blown away. All coherent thoughts about what to say next escaped him.

''I've been looking for you. I thought you left without saying goodbye.''

She took a step toward him and lightly touched his sleeve. ''I'm sorry we didn't get to talk more. There were so many people. I felt like a tennis ball, bouncing from one group to the next....'' She shook her head and laughed.

''I understand,'' Connor cut in. From the way it had looked to him, it was more like Todd pulling her around from group to group, like so much baggage. More than once, it had seemed to Connor that Laurel wanted a break from socializing, but Todd had forced her to press on. He didn't care if the man was her fiancé, Connor didn't like the way Todd Parson treated Laurel. She deserved so much better.

On impulse, he reached out and took her hand. She seemed surprised but pleased, and he felt the slight, answering pressure of her fingers responding to his. "I was wondering if you had any free time tomorrow. Maybe we could get together, have some coffee in town…maybe at that place with the fishnets on the ceiling? Do they still make their own doughnuts?"

"Sorry, that place went upscale. You can probably get a cappuccino and croissants, but they don't serve a good old, down-to-earth doughnut anymore," she reported wistfully.

"I've got a better idea. Why don't we go down to the beach near the landing? You know, where the sailboat ran into the rocks," Connor continued. There were so many special places he wanted to visit again with Laurel.

"Please, don't remind me," she laughed, and covered her mouth with her hand. "I was at the helm, remember. You were so sweet not to get angry with me about wrecking your boat," she teased him. "And so brave getting us back to shore."

"It was fun being shipwrecked with you." His reply was teasing and light. But his voice husky and rough.

As his dark gaze met hers and their bodies leaned a slight, but significant degree, closer, the moment suddenly changed to something far more intense, charged with the energy of their powerful attraction.

"I would love to see you tomorrow," Laurel said finally in a velvety, hushed voice. Her words and the way she gently squeezed his hand made his soul sing.

But just as she agreed to grant his heart's desire, Phillip appeared out of nowhere. "Better call it a night, Laurel. Don't you remember, you and Todd promised to come sailing tomorrow with me and Liza and her folks. Liza will be around to pick us up at seven, sharp. You won't be able to get up in time if you don't get some sleep," he whined.

"Oh, that's right." Laurel shook her head regretfully. "I do have plans, I guess. Maybe we won't be back that late though," she added hopefully.

Before Connor could reply, Phillip cut in again. "I wouldn't bet on it. Liza's father plans on sailing to some friends' house on the Vineyard."

Sounded as if they wouldn't get home until late tomorrow night. Especially if Phillip had anything to say about it. He was hovering over Laurel right now like a guard dog. Todd Parson's guard dog, Connor surmised. Those two probably got along well, cut from the same cloth.

"Well, some other time then," Connor said. He stared down at Laurel, his gaze conveying so much more than his polite words.

"Yes, some other time," she agreed, the regretful note in her voice cutting at his heart. "I'll be in the city soon. Maybe we can have lunch."

"Sure thing." Connor nodded. He swallowed back his disappointment. "Your father knows how to get in touch with me."

It was the polite thing to say, he knew. But it would never happen. Even if it did, by the time their next meeting came about, Laurel would most likely be Mrs. Todd Parson—and beyond his reach. Connor knew it would hurt too much to see her again after she married.

"Well, looks like it's hello and goodbye," Phillip said to Connor. "Bet it brought back memories for you, coming here."

"It did," Connor replied evenly. Though not all of them pleasant, he did not add. "Good night, Phillip," he said.

Then turning to Laurel, he gazed into her eyes and smiled. "Thanks for our dance," he said in a voice for her alone. She smiled at him, but before she could reply, he leaned down and quickly, lightly kissed her cheek. "Good luck, Laurel. I'm sorry I didn't come home to visit sooner," he added. "I would have given Parson a run for his money."

"Good night, Connor...." He felt Laurel's fleeting touch and heard her voice trail off as he continued to move away from her.

He strode across the patio with determined steps, weaving his way around the hired help who were now busily cleaning up the party debris. Finally, he was away from the bright lights, on a path through the garden that led to the front grounds, where he had parked his car.

The darkness and sudden quiet offered some comfort. He felt numb and empty. He felt as if his heart was breaking. How could he leave her? How could he just go without letting her know how he felt? This was his last chance. His only chance.

Still, he did not see that there was anything more he could do.

Maybe it was all for the best, Connor thought as he saw the lights at the end of the path. She didn't feel the same. The thought stung painfully, and yet, it had to be true.

If she did feel the same—if she felt even half of

what he felt for her right now—she would have given him some sign. She would have figured out some way to see him again. Even if she had to sail to the Vineyard tomorrow.

Even if she had to sail to China.

Was he fooling himself? Did he merely want what he couldn't have? He didn't think so. He wasn't that way about women usually. He wouldn't be that way about Laurel.

Laurel. Just as he'd come to realize what she meant to him, she was snatched out of reach. God, it hurt so much.

How long would he feel like this? Months, probably. Years, maybe.

Forever?

Connor found his car, one of the few left at the end of the long curving driveway. Even the valets, hired for the night, had gone home by now. His vision blurred, he fumbled in his pocket for the keys, then dropped his key ring on the gravel. Damn, he wasn't actually crying, was he? He hadn't cried since…he couldn't remember when.

He brushed his hand across the back of his damp eyes and took a deep, calming breath. He had to get away from here. He had to get off the Cape tomorrow, as early as possible. Maybe he'd pack up the car when he got home, rest a few hours and leave at dawn. Before Laurel even met up with her sailing party.

Deep in thought, Connor did not hear the light footsteps running down the driveway toward him. He didn't notice a sound until Laurel stood just steps away.

"Connor…wait," she called to him in a breathless, urgent whisper.

He turned and saw her, running toward him. He moved to meet her and instinctively opened his arms, his hands coming to rest on her slim waist. She stepped into his embrace, placing her hands on his broad chest and, for a moment, as she caught her breath, leaned her head down so that it fit just under his chin. He felt his lips and cheek brush against her silky hair before she lifted her head again. Thankfully, she did not move away.

"Laurel, what it is? What's the matter?"

"Thank goodness I caught you." She was winded from running, and holding her so close, he suddenly felt breathless, too. "I couldn't let you just go like that, Connor. It felt so…final," she tried to explain. "Too final," she added.

He nodded. He knew exactly what she meant. There was no need to explain. "I think we should talk. How about down at the beach?"

"But I'm busy tomorrow. That stupid sailing date with Phillip's future in-laws," she reminded him.

"Not tomorrow, tonight." His hands moved up to grip her smooth shoulders. "Right now," he said urgently.

As she gazed at him, he could read the flux and flow of indecision in her beautiful face—anticipation, desire, hesitation and guilt all flashed before his eyes. Her wide azure eyes studied him. Could she see that he'd been crying? God, he hoped not.

Finally, she nodded. "Wait for me by the dock. I'll be there in a little while."

He said nothing, just stared down at her as inexpressible feelings washed over him—relief, gratitude and then, a sweet rising wave of anticipation. She tenderly cupped his cheek with the palm of her hand.

Then an instant later, she turned and ran back up the driveway toward the dark shadow of the Sutherland mansion.

Connor made his way to the beach on a sandy path overgrown with bramble and vines. If he hadn't known the path existed, he would have never found it.

It was slow going. Luckily, a full moon had risen high in the clear night sky and the moonlight illuminated his steps. Finally, he came out at the Sutherlands' stretch of private beach. He slipped off his jacket and shoes and rolled up the cuffs of his trousers. He spotted a long driftwood log and sat on it, staring out at the sea, as good a place as any to wait. The waves moved toward the shore in a smooth, regular rhythm, the blue-black water rippling in the distance like a skein of satin.

He'd often come down here after dark with Laurel when they were young. They'd build a fire and tell spooky stories. More often than not, Charles Sutherland would come looking for Laurel and sit with them, telling stories of his own. He had some good ones. And just as they'd never given a thought to the future back then, right now, Connor could think of nothing but the past. A simpler time. A time when the golden summer days seemed to stretch on endlessly, without beginning or end, and every day was a new adventure.

And along with the images of the cloudless blue skies and long sunny days, always came the image of Laurel. Laurel, laughing, joking, confiding her secrets, her troubles, her dreams. Her tanned, slender arms and legs gracefully swinging as she strolled be-

side him on the smooth wet sand, her golden hair
waving behind her like a flag, her turquoise-blue eyes
sparkling, the way the sun danced on the waves. Her
wide, warm smile so accepting, so understanding. So
loving.

She still had that smile. She was still the same,
exactly, as she'd been—yet, now, so much more. He
swallowed hard, and looked up at the house. The yel-
low squares of light in each window had all gone
black. The caterer and cleanup crew were gone for
the night. Everyone in the mansion had gone to bed.

Laurel would be here soon.

He could barely wait to feel her in his arms. To
hold her and kiss her. To press his face into her soft
hair and tell her how beautiful she was. How he'd
never let her go now that he'd found her again.

He stood up, rubbing his hands together, searching
the ragged line of trees and brush for some sign of
her. He checked his watch. Barely ten minutes had
passed. It felt like ten hours.

He stared out at the water again, his hands on his
hips. The sound and motion of the surf was a soothing
distraction, calming him a bit.

Finally, he heard her soft footsteps on the sand behind him. He spun around just as she stood about an
arm's length away. Still dressed in her glamorous
gown, she'd removed all her jewelry—including her
engagement ring, he noticed—and her shoes. She'd
also removed the dressy clip that had held back the
side of her hair, and her wavy golden mane was now
blown back from her face by the breeze off the ocean.

He didn't say a word. Couldn't speak. He stepped
toward her and cupped her bare shoulders in his
hands. He pressed his cheek against her hair,

breathing in the rich, flowery scent of her hair and skin. Laurel moved smoothly into his embrace, her arms looping around his waist, her soft, full breasts pressed to his chest.

She stirred against him, murmured his name, and his arms moved down to encircle her, gripping her tightly to him. For a moment, Connor felt as if he might explode.

Then his hands went up to her hair and he lifted her face to his. Her eyes were huge, liquid blue, dark as the sea and churning with longing, a hunger to love and be loved. He felt her run her hands along the hard planes of his back as if to confirm the message that her eyes had already so eloquently expressed.

They had talking to do. They had important things to discuss, to decide. He needed to keep his head, act responsibly. Honorably. He didn't want Laurel to have regrets. Recriminations. He couldn't stand it if she ended up feeling that way.

He gazed down at her. About to say something. Anything. And yet, no words came. Finally, his head dipped to the irresistible lure of her moist, red lips. Their mouths met and merged, his kiss questioning at first. Then, as he felt her eager response, the kiss quickly deepened to a passionate expression of all Connor felt for her. And all Laurel felt for him.

Her hands glided over his muscular chest and shoulders, then around to his back again, boldly caressing him. Connor answered in kind, sweeping his hands down the curves of her lithe form, from her shoulders to her hips, then back up again, to gently cup her breasts, circling the hardened tips with the pads of his thumbs. Laurel's kiss felt wild against his mouth for a moment before she softly moaned with pleasure, her body sagging helplessly against him.

"You're so beautiful," he whispered in a husky voice. "You take my breath away."

Moments later, they dropped onto the sand. As their kisses grew wilder and even more intense, Connor cushioned Laurel's head with one strong arm, the other stroking her from hip to thigh. His mouth moved from her lips, down the column of her throat and across the silky skin exposed by the low neckline of her gown. With his fingertip and tongue he teased and tasted the sensitive flesh at the top of her cleavage and soon had loosened the zipper at the back enough to pull the fabric down, exposing her breasts to his passionate touch.

He felt Laurel's fingers moving through his thick hair as his mouth covered one rosy, sensitive nipple. She moaned and stirred under him, pressing her hips provocatively against his. He was sure that she must have felt his readiness for her, his throbbing need to make them one. He took a deep, ragged breath and lifted his head to look down at her. Her eyes were half-closed, dazed with passion, her gorgeous face flushed, her glorious hair splayed out around her head like a cloud of spun gold.

"Laurel. Darling," he whispered. He kissed her lightly and then swallowed hard. "If you want me to stop, now's the time to say it."

She framed his face with her cool, soft hands and looked deeply into his eyes. "I want you, Connor. I want to make love with you. Please."

His pulse beat madly out of control as her words penetrated his fevered brain. Her thrilling caresses had set a fire burning inside him that burst out of control. He struggled to repress an instinctive impulse to plunge himself into her body at his next breath. As he held still above her, trying to slow himself down, her fingers nimbly opened his shirt buttons and he felt her warm mouth moving over his chest, kissing him, tasting him, her warm, wet tongue swirling around his sensitive nipple.

He felt his body shudder and he moved to rest on his side in the sand, as Laurel's caresses moved lower, her mouth tenderly exploring his flat abdomen, her hands caressing his chest and then his thighs. He felt her unfasten his belt and the top of his pants, then felt her hand slip inside his pants to cup and caress his male hardness, stroking him until he thought he'd cry out with the unbearably intense pleasure of her touch.

When Connor knew he could stand no more of her seductive caresses, he raised himself above her again, his hand sliding up under her gown, up her smooth, strong leg. His fingertips found the lacy edge of her panties and his fingers slipped inside, seeking and finding her slick velvety warmth. He could feel that she was more than ready for him. But he wanted to make this perfect for her, he wanted to thrill her in a way no other man ever had before.

His fingers expertly stroking the peak of her pulsing womanhood, Connor was alert to the slightest shift of her body, the slightest change in her breathing, eager to please her, to touch her exactly as she wanted. His mouth moved again to her breast, sucking and soothing her nipples. Laurel fell back against the sand, sighing and writhing with pleasure as his masterful loving pushed her higher and higher.

She gripped his powerful shoulders, her hips thrusting up to meet the lovingly slow strokes of his hand.

He felt her shiver and press her face into the hollow between his neck and shoulder. She took a deep, shuddering breath and pressed herself close to him.

"Connor, please. Come to me," she said. "I can't wait anymore." With her hands on his hips, she gently urged his body to cover her own.

"Neither can I, sweetheart," he whispered. With his mouth pressed to her own, Connor hastily pushed her gown up over her hips and settled between her thighs. Moments later, he made their bodies one.

He heard Laurel's sharply indrawn breath and felt her body tense, then tremble in his arms. He held very still, kissing her hair until he felt her relax again beneath him. When he began to move slowly inside her, he heard her moan deep and low at the back of her throat, but it was a sound of pure pleasure and it thrilled him, inspiring him to move even deeper, to give her even more.

Their bodies moved as one in an ageless rhythm, an echo of the steady pounding of the waves against the shoreline. Connor thrust faster and deeper, every sigh and movement of Laurel's hips rising to meet his own, driving him wild with passion for her.

She was indescribably beautiful, unique and precious, the rarest treasure he'd ever know. As he brought her to a climax of pleasure and felt himself reaching his own, some dim, distant part of his mind felt as if this moment of complete possession had not served to satisfy one single drop of his hunger for her. To the contrary, to love her, to hold and have her this way had opened a door in his heart, or even his soul, that had been long left locked and sealed. But now it stood open, leading to a road of limitless longing for her—a need for her that would never be satisfied, never sated.

Just as he heard Laurel's cries of ecstasy as she reached her peak, he felt himself topple over the edge. He shuddered in her arms and felt her tremble beneath him. Their mouths merged in a deep, devouring kiss as Connor moved within her with one last powerful thrust. He felt her shiver and grip him close, hearing her call his name as her body clenched around him, and they cleaved together in the ultimate of intimacy, as close as two beings could ever be.

Some time later, Connor and Laurel sat together in a close embrace, leaning back on the driftwood log. He had covered her with his suit jacket and then wrapped her possessively in his arms. Her head rested on his chest, tucked below his chin, her arms loped around his waist as he stroked her hair.

He stared up at the stars, still too moved to speak. Finally he said, "Tell me you won't marry Todd Parson. I don't think I could stand it if you did."

"No, I can't marry him," Laurel agreed softly. She looked up at him and touched her hand to his cheek. "Right now, I can't even remember why I wanted to."

Two

Seven years later

Laurel glanced at the small gold clock on her desk. Nine thirty-three. Barely two minutes had passed since she'd last checked, though somehow, it felt like two hours. Connor Northrup was due to arrive at ten o'clock. She would not go down to the meeting room until then.

She felt the flurry of butterflies churning her stomach and tried to ignore it. She turned her attention to her desktop, piled with papers, and tried to focus on the task at hand, trying to determine if Sutherland Enterprises should sue a supplier who had failed to keep to the terms of their contract.

Laurel flipped open a folder of correspondence and tried to concentrate on the stack of letters. Some were quite old, dated up to five years ago and signed with her former married name, Laurel Parson.

She didn't like to be reminded of her marriage. She felt a wave of sadness, futile sadness, actually. When her friends and family had heard the story of Todd's infidelity, they had naturally rushed to support her, to make Todd out to be the villain of the piece.

But Laurel knew better. It took two to make a mess of a marriage and she had played her part.

The truth was, she should have never married Todd in the first place.

The truth was, she had been unfaithful to him even before they'd spoken their vows.

One clear-cut act of betrayal with her body, on a moonlit beach—and after that, years of betrayal in her heart, believing herself to be irrevocably in love with a man who had simply used her to fulfill some long-simmering fantasy. A man who had promised her the world, and asked—no, *demanded*—that she turn her entire world upside down for him with a snap of his fingers.

Then…nothing. Not a word. Not a card. Not a single phone call.

So, she had gone through with her marriage, come back to reality, she thought. Fulfilled her promises, her responsibility, though she knew all along her heart wasn't in it. And, unfortunately, neither was the rest of her body, she reflected. For although she had given herself to Connor with bold abandon, she'd never responded to Todd with anything close to that degree of passion and sensuality.

Todd had accused her of being cold. Frigid. That was the reason he'd needed to wander. It was really all her fault, according to Todd. She'd accepted the accusation without argument, for how could she dare explain why she knew it wasn't true? Besides, she did feel guilty about her lack of passion for him. About the light of love that had burned in her heart for another man, for so many years, unseen and unrequited.

Yes, discovering Todd's affair had been painful and humiliating. But the pain had been nothing compared with the sense of loss and betrayal she'd felt, the humiliation of being played for a fool, when Connor Northrup had used her for a one-night stand.

What other explanation was there for what had happened? If Connor Northrup had the nerve to offer one, she knew she'd refuse to believe it.

She had almost expected to see him at her father's funeral two years ago. But Connor had been traveling on business at the time and had sent a note of sympathy along with a staggering arrangement of flowers. Her father had adored Connor. Taken a deep interest in him as a boy and helped him fulfill his potential as a young man. After Connor entered the work world, Charles had kept in touch with him, bragged about his successes as if Connor had been his own son. Sometimes she thought he liked him even more than Phillip.

Why should it matter so much after all this time? Laurel shook her head, silently scolding herself. She should know better by now. She should at least act as if she did. And, in about ten minutes, she would do exactly that. She would act as if it didn't matter and had never mattered to her, in fact. She would put on such a convincing show of cool, polite, business-like persona that even Connor Northrup would not dare to bring up the past.

She dreaded this meeting. She had dreaded this day

ever since Laurel had learned that the firm that handled Sutherland's annual audit had merged with a group of financial analysts headed by Connor Northrup. But now it had come—the day that they would meet again, face-to-face.

She remembered how handsome he was. Remembered much too well, in fact. She knew it was mean of her, but she hoped he'd lost his hair, or gotten a big potbelly. Or both. It had been seven years since she'd seen him. Anything could have happened. He might be married, with ten kids, for all she knew. She found herself frowning at the thought, then shook her head.

Laurel gave up on trying to review the old letters and pushed the pile of papers back into the folder. She rose from the desk and walked into the private bathroom that adjoined her office. She rinsed her hands, then quickly checked her appearance. *Just as I would do before any other meeting of this kind,* Laurel assured herself. She was not making any special effort for Connor Northrup. Still, she could not help wondering if he would find her appearance changed. She knew she had changed since that summer night years ago. People remarked on it. Or held themselves back from remarking on it, she had noticed.

Her body was basically the same—if anything she'd gotten a bit thinner. The expensive, high-style navy blue suit she had chosen for today with its sleek, severe cut certainly made her look model thin. The color complemented her fair hair. Her hair was still long, though she rarely wore it down anymore, and certainly not at the office. Today it was swept up in a sophisticated style. Her pearl earrings added to the elegant, businesslike image.

Her eyes—which Connor had once rhapsodized over—were still blue, she noted with a wry smile. But she was older and wiser and it showed, she knew. The sparkle was gone, replaced by a certain accepting dullness. Maturity, some might call it. But at that moment, Laurel wondered if it couldn't more accurately be called cynicism. Bitterness. The shadow of vain hopes.

Silly thoughts. Useless thoughts, really. She couldn't let Connor guess that she had any feelings about seeing him at all. After all, she did have her self-respect.

She'd never worn much makeup. Never needed to, and now, even when a bit of blush or concealer for the shadows under her eyes might have helped, she didn't want to bother. She applied fresh lipstick in a brisk, efficient motion and snapped the tube closed.

She was as ready as she'd ever be. She checked her watch. Five to ten. Time to head down to the conference room near Phillip's office.

Laurel grabbed her leather-bound notepad and a pen off her desk. When she left her office, she gave instructions to her assistant, Emily, then headed down the long hallway. The dark green carpeting was thick and her steps were nearly soundless.

It was almost a relief to get it over with, Laurel reflected. She hoped that Connor would keep the discussion brief and focused on business matters. Business matters he clearly thought were urgent, but didn't see fit to illuminate or explain when he'd called Phillip last night to arrange this meeting.

Something having to do with the company's annual

outside audit, she assumed. The audit that was reported each year to Sutherland Enterprises's board of
directors. She knew it was presently taking place, but
hadn't heard of any significant problem or questions.
Phillip hadn't mentioned any.

At least she wouldn't be alone with him. Phillip
would be there. Recalling how Connor and her
brother got along about as well as oil and water, she
wondered if Phillip's presence would be any help. He
would, at the very least, deflect some of Connor's
attention.

After her father's death, Phillip had been named
CEO and taken over the helm. Even Laurel had to
admit that he had not been doing a stellar job in the
post, despite the fact that he had been groomed for
years for the role, Laurel reflected as she boarded the
elevator and punched the button for the ninth floor.

Phillip was not a good manager and was often quite
impulsive, without enough patience to learn about all
the facts and consider them carefully before making
important decisions. Phillip was shrewd, Laurel
thought, but not truly intelligent. Certainly not wise
about people, as her father had been, which to Laurel
was the essence of running any business, really.

It was all a soft soap, diplomatic way of saying that
Phillip was not up to the job. And the financial health
of the company would eventually suffer. Had already
suffered, she feared. But it was a demanding position.
She truly hoped that it was merely a matter of time
before her brother grew into his role.

Laurel got off the elevator and walked down to the
conference room near her brother's large corner office. When she opened the door, she was surprised to

find that Phillip was already there, waiting. Like some reigning monarch, it was usually his habit to make everyone assemble for a meeting and have them sit waiting for him before he swept in and took his seat at the head of the table.

But there he was, waiting for Connor Northrup. Like a boy who had misbehaved, waiting for the principal, was Laurel's immediate impression. But that was silly. Why should Phillip feel nervous about meeting with Connor? She was the one who had reason to feel nervous. If anything, Phillip should feel he had the upper hand in such a meeting.

"Laurel, there you are. I was just about to call your office," Phillip said as she walked in. "Come in. Come in," he urged her. "Don't forget to shut the door."

She closed the door behind her and took a seat near him. He sat drumming a pencil nervously on the tabletop. He stared off into space and barely seemed to notice her. His immaculate white shirt, flamboyant silk tie and finely tailored suit couldn't make up for his depleted physical appearance. Bloated and pale, with dark circles under his eyes, he didn't look well, she thought. The long hours and responsibilities were catching up with him. She knew full well how her father had shielded Phillip from the heavy lifting, even toward the end. But now he was left to handle it all on his own, without Charles to turn to for advice or support. The effort was taking a toll.

"You don't look well, Phillip," she said bluntly. "Are you worried about something? Something about the audit?"

He stared at her. She thought for a moment he was about to open up to her, to disclose the reason for the anxious—almost desperate—look that flashed across his face. Then, in the blink of an eye, she saw his expression change, return to a remote, impassive mask.

"No, there's nothing wrong," he replied finally. "I do have a headache though. A bad one. Must be the air in this office. No one can ever seem to get it right."

He dropped the pencil and rubbed his forehead with his fingertips. His knuckles were white, she noticed, his fingernails bitten down to the nub. He'd always had that nervous habit. Their mother had tried everything to break him of it, including bitter-tasting liquid she'd patiently paint on Phillip's fingers.

She wished he would confide in her more, use her as a sounding board. She knew this business as well as anyone. But she always sensed that Phillip kept her—and other principals in the company—in the dark about many things. Maybe it was a just a male thing, she reflected. Not wanting to look weak by asking for help.

"Are you sure, Phillip? You can tell me, you know, if there's some problem brewing," she said gently. "In confidence, I mean."

"There's nothing," he snapped irritably. He threw his hands down on the smooth, polished tabletop, his palms flat so that they made a sharp sound. A sound that made Laurel jerk back in her seat. "I just told you. I have a headache. Why do you keep nagging me?"

Laurel looked at him squarely, then shifted her gaze to the window. He took a deep breath and sat up straighter in his seat. When he was composed again, he said, "Sorry, Laurel. I know you mean well.

I'm just edgy this morning. Didn't sleep well, then had too much coffee to wake up, I guess.''

''It's okay.'' she replied. Obviously, for some reason, the prospect of seeing Connor Northrup again had upset her brother's peace of mind as well.

Phillip checked his watch. ''Where the hell is Northrup anyway? I can't waste my entire morning waiting for him.''

As if on cue, the conference-room phone at Phillip's side buzzed and he quickly answered it. ''Good, send him in,'' Laurel heard him say.

''He's here. Finally,'' Phillip said as he set the phone back in the cradle. He ran his hands through his hair and straightened his tie, then took a pose in his chair that might have had the caption Corporate Leader inscribed below, Laurel thought.

She licked her lips nervously, feeling her pulse go into overdrive, but she hoped to maintain an air of composure.

A moment later, the door swung open and Connor Northrup's tall, commanding figure appeared.

He had changed very little from that summer night long ago, Laurel thought. Except to have filled out a bit. Matured. And to have grown even more handsome in the process, she forced herself to acknowledge.

She watched, barely breathing, as his dark gaze swept around the room, falling first on her brother. ''Phillip,'' Connor said with a nod.

''Good morning, Northrup. Come in. Take a seat,'' Phillip replied with an expansive gesture of his arm. ''We've been waiting for you.''

Connor entered with smooth, confident strides and

took the seat directly opposite Laurel. He sat down and she had no choice but to meet his gaze.

"Hello, Connor," she greeted him in what she hoped was an easy, impersonal tone.

"Laurel. Good to see you again," he greeted her quietly. Politely. Yet his dark gaze captured hers with a compelling intensity.

Laurel felt a warm flush rising up her neck and into her cheeks. She averted her gaze to the notepad in front of her and jotted down the date and subject of the meeting with a trembling hand.

He was still so very handsome. More handsome than any man had a right to be, she thought. If anything, the years had improved him, made his dark looks even more rugged and masculine. And now he had even more confidence and self-assurance, which added to his appeal.

This meeting was going to be far harder for her than she had imagined, Laurel realized. But there was nothing she could do but sit tight and stick it out.

"We knew that your firm had merged with Delaney and Barton," Phillip said, naming the accounting firm that had served Sutherland Enterprises for decades. "But I didn't think we'd rate such exclusive attention. By the head of the place, no less."

Connor ignored Phillip's jocular manner and his tone was very serious when he answered. "As I told you last night, Phillip, some disturbing information has come to my attention having to do with the audit."

Laurel's gaze flew from Connor to Phillip.

So her brother had lied to her. He'd told her that he had no idea why Connor wanted to meet with them. She looked at Phillip, but he averted his gaze.

He knew she wouldn't embarrass him by calling him on this. Not in front of Connor.

When she looked again at Connor, she could tell that in that split second all was clear to him. Nothing had changed. Phillip was still misleading her, lying to her, tangling her in his deceptive webs. Connor's look was sympathetic, she thought. But it was sympathy she didn't want. Not from him.

"Yes, yes," Phillip said impatiently. "So you said last night. Why don't you just tell us what you've come up with, Northrup?"

"In a moment," Connor replied calmly. "I've prepared something for you both. Some information I think you ought to see."

He opened his fine leather briefcase and withdrew two manila folders, then passed one to Phillip and one across the table to Laurel. As he completed his task, she saw the tight set of Connor's jaw and sensed the war waging within as he struggled to keep his temper under control. Phillip was acting particularly nasty this morning. Like a frightened, cornered animal, she thought. Was it merely Connor that had set him off? Or was there something more?

Phillip didn't even touch his folder. In fact, he pushed it away, then slumped back in his chair with an exasperated sigh.

Laurel flipped hers open and looked down at a spreadsheet of figures. Part of the auditor's report, she assumed.

"You don't need to read these through now," Connor explained. "I just wanted you to have the proof in hand for what I'm about to say. Just in case there's any...denial."

Proof? Denial? Laurel didn't like the sound of the

words. In fact, as an attorney, such terminology set off alarm bells. "Has there been some wrongdoing? Some discrepancies in the numbers?"

She looked to Connor for an answer. He hesitated to speak. His eyes were wide, beseeching her to understand what he had come to do. To forgive him, even. To forgive him for…what?

Then Connor said to her, "It looks serious, Laurel. Very serious. But perhaps there's some explanation. That's why I've come to you and Phillip privately this way."

"Oh, God." Phillip gasped. "What did I do to deserve this?" He laughed out loud. A chilling, almost hysterical sound, Laurel thought. "And Connor Northrup, of all people, my judge and jury. And they say God doesn't have a sense of humor." He shook his head, half laughing, half weeping.

Laurel turned to him. She felt her heartbeat race. Something awful was happening here.

"Phillip? What is it? Tell me, please," she urged him.

"No, no…" His voice trailed off. He covered his face with his hands. He was crying now, real tears. "Let him tell you," he screamed angrily, pointing his finger at Connor. "That's why he's come after all. Let's not steal his hour of glory."

Connor sat erect in his seat, a stone-cold expression on his face. Laurel watched as he stared down at the folder that sat before him on the table and tapped it once with his fingertips. He lifted his dark head and looked at Phillip. His mouth was a tight line, his eyes narrowed, his gaze hardened. He was untouched by Phillip's malicious words, Laurel thought. Or, if Phillip had stung, Connor managed ably to hide it, maintaining an air of complete authority and rationality that made him appear leagues above the other man.

"I can step out of the room for a moment, if you like, Phillip. So that you can compose yourself."

"No, go on. I want to get this over with. The sooner the better."

Phillip took a deep breath and sat up in his chair. He took a hankie from his pocket and blew his nose. Laurel felt sick to her stomach. She had a strong intuition about what was coming but didn't want to hear the words spoken aloud. She didn't want to face the inevitable painful truth.

"It appears that large sums of money have been removed without authorization from Sutherland accounts. Particularly from the employee retirement fund," Connor explained in a dispassionate tone. "It appears that there has been some attempt to cover up the withdrawals. However, after investigating the discrepancies, the paper trail leads back to Phillip."

Laurel gasped. She felt the room spin.

Her gaze swept from Connor to her brother, who sat rigidly in his seat, his face without expression, his hands gripping the arms of his leather chair, as if preparing to take a blow.

"Oh, Phillip," she said with a deep sigh. She shook her head as the image of her brother was blurred by the tears that welled up in her eyes.

She didn't have to ask if Connor's accusation was true. She knew, deep in her heart, that it was. Just as she could now see so many little signs during the last few months that something wrong was going on, right under her nose. She saw the signals but failed to put the pieces together. Or, maybe more likely, she denied it to herself.

Laurel quickly wiped her eyes on a tissue, took a deep breath and willed herself to regain control. The entire situation was a nightmare—and Connor Northrup's role made it her worst nightmare.

"How much money is involved?" Laurel asked him.

Connor named a staggering figure and Laurel felt the wind knocked out of her.

"Of course, that's just a preliminary total. I haven't quite finished my investigation."

Phillip laughed harshly. "Well, you've damn well finished me off, Northrup. I suppose you feel very proud of that, don't you? Look at him preening, would you?" he urged Laurel. "He can hardly keep the smirk off his face."

Connor's expression could hardly be called preening, Laurel thought. Nor did he appear to be wearing a smirk. As he looked at Phillip's cowering figure, it was more a look of pity. A look that made Laurel feel deeply ashamed for her brother.

"This must feel good, Northrup." Phillip carped bitterly. "The servant's boy finally bringing down the almighty Sutherlands. You've waited a lifetime for this, haven't you?" he snarled.

"Phillip, that's enough," Laurel said curtly.

"Enough? I've barely gotten started!" Phillip snapped.

Laurel was about to urge him to control his temper, when Connor spoke first.

"Let him speak, Laurel. He has something to say to me. Let him say it." Connor's deep, authoritative tone commanded her full attention.

"How noble of you, Northrup. Let the condemned man speak," Phillip mocked. "You bastard—when I think of all my father did for you, it turns my stomach to see you here today. So high and mighty now, aren't you? You would have been nothing without his help. You'd have been pumping gas someplace out in the boondocks. A common laborer, with grease under your fingernails and without two bills in your pocket to rub together. Just like your old man," he ranted. "My father made you what you are today. You owe him, Northrup. Big time. Is this how you repay your debts?" he asked incredulously. "By destroying everything my father ever loved—his business *and* his family?

"Phillip!" Laurel burst out finally. She couldn't bear to hear another word of his acrimonious assault. As if Connor was the one to blame here!

Connor had been staring straight ahead during the entire outburst, as if waiting out a child's tantrum. He now turned his eyes toward Phillip.

"Despite what you may think, Phillip, and despite our disagreements in the past, it has distressed me to deliver this news. It's made me truly unhappy," he stated, his tone firm but sincere. "Since I discovered this mess, I've thought of little else than my friendship with your father. And my friendship with both of you," he added in a somewhat strained voice.

He looked up at Laurel briefly and their gazes met for a heart-stopping second. Images of the passion they'd shared flashed through her mind.

She knew beyond question that at that instant he was remembering, too. She felt her cheeks warm with color and stared down at her hands.

Friendship, he'd called it.

A message to her perhaps that if she'd had any

doubt left at all about his feelings for her, either then or now, he was putting a label on them for her.

"I know what your father stood for, Phillip. I know what he believed in," Connor continued. "He believed in honesty. In taking the right way, not the easy way. No matter what you think, it hasn't been easy, or pleasurable for me in any way to come here today. If there's any good in this situation at all, perhaps it's the fact that I was the one to make this discovery and not a stranger. Not someone who would have taken this whole matter directly to your board and to the legal authorities."

"Always so noble, Northrup. So much better than the rest of us, aren't you?" Phillip chided. "Yes, you're doing me a great favor, aren't you?"

"You've said enough, Phillip," Laurel reprimanded him. "More than enough," she added.

Didn't Phillip realize it would hurt his case even more to keep playing these childish games? Besides, she needed to get all the facts, as legal counsel for the firm and as a company principal. Maybe there was some way out of this mess. There had to be.

"So no one else knows about this?" Laurel asked Connor. "Only you?"

He nodded. "An accountant supervising the audit came to me when he found the first small problem. I took the project over from him and kept digging on my own. I've managed so far to keep it to myself. In fact, if you can figure out how to replace the missing money, no one but us three need ever know," he promised her.

Laurel's gaze lingered on Connor's concerned expression. A thick lock of his dark hair had fallen across his forehead. He carelessly brushed it back with his hand. Despite everything, despite her long, painful nights and bitter feelings of betrayal, she could still see what had drawn her to him. What still drew her to him. There was so much good in him. He had a strong, protective nature. He was someone to instinctively turn to when there was trouble. He was a kind man, too, she believed, a person who didn't enjoy causing anyone else pain.

So why had he caused her so much heartache years ago? Was there some explanation? An explanation even she hadn't considered yet? Couldn't imagine?

Laurel pushed the errant thought aside, forcing her mind to focus on the current crisis. And forced her gaze to pull away from Connor's sympathetic dark eyes.

"That is a generous offer. But I'm not at all sure Phillip and I can raise that much money," she answered honestly.

"Not sure? I'm sure. It's impossible," Phillip wailed. "Just impossible."

Laurel turned away from her brother and looked again at Connor. "If we can't repay the missing funds, you'll no doubt take action," she added, the words difficult to say aloud.

"I don't see that I have any other choice," Connor replied evenly.

"Yes, I understand." Laurel swallowed hard. She could hear Phillip quietly weeping, his head hidden in his hands, his anger spent for now. She didn't have the heart—or perhaps the stomach—to even look at him.

How would the board react? They would have Phillip arrested. He'd go to jail, she had no doubt. And what of herself? Would they suspect that she was involved as well? Or knew what was going on before today? Laurel shuddered to consider the possibility. She would probably have to prove that she was innocent. But innocent or not, her law career would be ruined.

There would be a scandal, news stories. The family name dragged through the mud. The company would go under. All her father's hard work, the work of his lifetime, and of his father before him, sent up in smoke.

She would survive somehow, she always had. But what of Phillip? What of his wife and children, innocent victims in this tragedy?

As Laurel's thoughts raced, she sighed out loud without even realizing it.

"Laurel?" Connor called quietly. She looked up to see him leaning toward her across the polished table. "I can keep this quiet for a few more days. I can't promise more than that, but it's something. Maybe by then you and Phillip will find some way to replace the money."

"Maybe," she replied numbly.

If Phillip was stealing money from the company, she would assume that his personal finances were a mess and that he was in deep debt. No help there. That left her only her own holdings to draw upon. She would have to sell her apartment or borrow against the equity, and cash in her investments and savings. She could sell off her possessions, items she'd inherited—antiques, paintings, jewelry. But it still wouldn't be enough money. She had a trust fund. But her father had been a very conservative man in such matters and she didn't have access to it until her thirtieth birthday. Two years from now. Even if she could get a loan against the trust, it still wouldn't be enough.

There was the summer place on the Cape that she now owned jointly with Phillip. But hadn't her father taken a huge loan against that property at some point, when he needed to raise capital to expand?

Laurel's mind was sent spinning with calculations. Her confusion must have shown on her face. She looked up to find Connor staring at her.

For a moment, he appeared as if he was about to say something else. Something more personal. She saw his hand stir, as if moved by the impulse to reach out to her. Then, having second thoughts, she saw him pull back, resuming his businesslike demeanor. He rose from his chair and grabbed his case.

"I realize this is a shock for you, Laurel. A shock for both of you," he added, glancing at Phillip. "You can call me if you have any questions, or need to talk more," he added. "Anytime."

He handed her his business card, and when she glanced down she noticed that he'd jotted his home phone number on the back.

"Yes, if we have any questions, we'll call," she replied. The same way she might have replied had this been any other ordinary business meeting. Not one that had devastated her life in the blink of an eye.

With a curt nod of his dark head, Connor turned and left the room. She heard the heavy door closing behind him.

Laurel stared blankly into space. What to do next? What to do? She glanced over at Phillip. With his head in his arms on the tabletop, his back shook with his deep sobs.

She rose and walked over to him, then touched his

shoulder. "Phillip, please," she urged him. "We need to talk."

"What more is there to say?" he replied, lifting his head. "Northrup is out for blood. He doesn't want to help us. He came here to drag it out, to torture me."

Laurel knew that there was no use arguing with him. Phillip was hysterical, irrational. He'd somehow turned this all around so that, from his point of view, Connor was completely to blame for the crisis they now faced. When, in fact, Laurel knew that what Connor had said was true, it had been extremely fortunate—an amazing coincidence, in fact—that Connor had been the one to discover Phillip's crime. At least it bought them a little time.

"Phillip, I need to ask you a few questions," Laurel began gently. Then, in her methodical, lawyerly way, she managed to drag the whole story from him, bit by bit.

He'd never liked the business, he confessed, and once their father had died and he'd taken over as CEO, he'd been desperate to get out. He had known all along he'd never spend the rest of his life heading up a company that manufactured heavy equipment for agriculture and the construction industry. What kind of a life was that? he asked her. It was acceptable to our father, she wanted to reply, who was as fine a man as she'd ever known. But she didn't interrupt him.

In order to leave the business, he needed money, he explained. Lots of money, considering the lifestyle he and his wife, Liza, needed to support. He didn't want to take another job, ever. Besides, who would hire him? Phillip knew his limits, his liabilities. His father had been easy on him, but a stranger wouldn't be. So in order to leave Sutherland Enterprises, he'd need quite a bit of money. Millions, actually. So much money, he'd never need to work another day in his life. That was his goal, his fantasy.

Phillip had used his trust fund—and a considerable sum of money his wife had brought to their marriage, as well—to back some high-risk investments, which he'd been told would yield huge returns.

Within months, he'd lost all he'd invested. Desperate to recoup, he'd gone into debt. Still, he could never catch up. He hoped to simply "borrow" the money from the firm's accounts, then replace it.

"I never thought of it as stealing, Laurel. Honestly," he swore to her as his tears of self-pity started to fall again. "I was going to pay it back. Every cent. In time."

Laurel considered a number of sarcastic remarks in reply, then bit them back. Her brother was weak. She'd always known that. She was blazing angry at him, but still, he was her brother, the only family she had left now, and she had to stand by him. No matter what.

Just as she suspected, he was completely in debt. When she asked if he thought his wife's parents might help him, he laughed out loud. "They hate my guts. They never wanted Liza to marry me. When they hear about this, they'll throw a party. They'll persuade Liza to divorce me. I'd bet anything on it."

Laurel sighed. "I can scrape up some of it," she offered. "But we'll still be far short of the figure needed," she said honestly. She then reviewed her assets with him and saw his expression grow bleaker and bleaker as it became clear that there seemed to be no way out.

Finally, she said, "I'll do everything I can to help you, Phillip. We'll hire the best attorney we can find. Perhaps we can prove that the stress of Dad's death and taking over the firm was simply too much for you. You weren't thinking clearly. You weren't in a stable state of mind…"

"The old insanity plea, you mean?" He laughed harshly. "Oh, that should look good on my résumé," he joked. Then he grabbed Laurel's hand and squeezed it so tightly she stifled a cry of pain. "I don't think I can face it, Laurel. The scandal. Prison…" He gulped, his red-rimmed eyes bulging. "I'll kill myself first. I swear it."

"Phillip! Don't even say such a thing. I know it all looks horrible right now, but we'll get through it. I promise. One step at a time," Laurel assured him.

Her words of comfort sounded meager, even to her own ears. Phillip, in prison? Even the prospect of spending a few years in a minimum-security prison for white-collar criminals might be enough to push her brother over the edge. To make him carry through on his suicide threat, Laurel thought as fear took a cold grip on her heart.

"Think of Liza," she whispered urgently. "Think of Scott and Lily," she urged, naming her five-year-old nephew and three-year-old niece.

"I am thinking of them," he sobbed quietly. "I'm thinking how much they'll hate me when they find out what I've done."

"Oh, Phillip, they won't hate you. They love you. They'll want to help you," she replied, hoping with all her heart that her words were true. She bit her lower lip. In truth, Laurel wasn't sure how Liza would react to such dreadful news—if she'd rise to the moment and stand by Phillip's side, or leave him flat. Liza had never impressed her as very forgiving or forbearing. But how many relationships could withstand such an ultimate test of loyalty?

"There's no one to help me," Phillip argued in a wretched, desperate voice. He tossed his head and pounded his fists on the tabletop. "No one, I tell you."

"I'm here, Phillip." Laurel sat in the chair nearest to him and took his fisted hand in both of her own. "I'll do anything I can. Honestly."

Phillip covered his tear-swollen face with his free hand, then looked at her. "You have to go to Connor Northrup. You have to get him to hide this mess somehow. These number crunchers, they know all the tricks, believe me. He could do it if he wanted to. Talk him into it. Strike a deal. You're so good at negotiating, at dealing with people. Dad should have left you in charge. Not me. I've made a mess of everything I ever laid my hand to," Phillip murmured.

"Talk to Connor?" Laurel sat back and stared at him. "How can I persuade him to do such a thing? You heard what he said. We have a little time to pay back the missing money. Then he'll go to the board."

"He can be persuaded otherwise. Believe me. Every man can be persuaded if you make the right offer. And he's always had a sweet spot for you," Phillip insisted. "I could see it today, in his eyes. He's still got a thing for you. He always did. And don't pretend you don't know what I mean, Laurel. He'll do whatever you say. If you ask him the right way," he added in a tone that made Laurel's skin crawl. And her blood boil.

She stood up abruptly. "Don't be ridiculous, Phil-

lip. I can't listen to another word of this...this gar-
bage. Any friendship I had with Connor Northrup is
ancient history. You're just grasping at straws now.
Understandably, but—''

''But what?'' he yelled at her. ''My life is literally
hanging by a thread here, Laurel. All I ask is one
simple, small favor and you refuse me, just like that.''
He snapped his fingers in her face. ''I know it's a
long shot. We're none of us getting any younger here,
that's for sure,'' he added as his gaze swept over her
in a way that stung her vanity. ''But for God's sake,
can't you see how desperate I am? Can't you just go
and talk to him? If not for me, think of my family,''
he begged her.

Laurel took a deep breath. ''All right. I'll call him
and set up another meeting. But I warn you, don't
expect anything more to come out of it than what you
heard him tell both of us today.''

''It can work, Laurel. Believe me, just do your part
and it will work like a charm.''

And what part was that? Seduce Connor Northrup,
she was sure was her brother's thinly veiled impli-
cation. Prostitute herself to save her brother's thin
skin.

If he only knew the absurdity of his plan. The truth
of the situation was so far from his fantasy, it was
laughable, really. Even if she was willing to try such
a ploy—which she certainly was not—the effort
would be futile.

But she couldn't dash Phillip's last hope. And she
wouldn't have it on her conscience years from now
that she refused this last—though hopeless—request.

Three

As Laurel's taxi stopped in front of Connor's apartment building, she once again regretted agreeing to a meeting at his home. Connor seemed to think that it would be easier somehow to talk there. Easier for whom? she'd wanted to reply. Certainly not her.

He also thought it would be more private than a meeting at either of their offices, or at a restaurant. That was true enough. But being alone with Connor was exactly what she dreaded.

As the taxi pulled away, she stood on the curb and flipped up the collar on her coat. A chilling wind blew off the nearby Hudson River. Strands of her long hair that had come loose from her upswept hairdo blew across her eyes. She brushed them back and stared up at the impressive facade of Connor's building. It appeared to have been a warehouse once upon a time, but as was common for the trendy downtown neighborhood, the building had been renovated to all of its former glory—and then some. It was an interesting area of town, where huge old buildings like this one that housed million-dollar apartments stood side by side to meatpacking plants. And ultraexpensive restaurants and art galleries shared the same block as warehouses and factories. She wouldn't have guessed that Connor would choose this area of the city to live. Though she could well remember his rebellious, unconventional side, the choice still seemed out of synch with the buttoned-down, executive persona he now put forward.

Well, people change, Laurel reminded herself as she entered the lobby. And sometimes they just aren't what you think in the first place. When she gave her name to the doorman, he appeared to be expecting her. As she walked toward the elevators, her anxious thoughts were distracted by the interesting metal sculptures and large contemporary paintings that decorated the common areas.

Of course, she had to agree to whatever time and location he suggested. He held all the cards in his hand and they both knew it. No matter how professional or even proud she tried to appear, she was still the supplicant, coming here to negotiate a deal—to beg for mercy, actually. From Phillip's perspective, she might even be coming here tonight to trade sexual favors for clemency. If Phillip only knew the position he was putting her into now. Laurel shook her head to clear away the worrisome thoughts.

It would do no good to keep thinking about the past—the way Connor had used her, hurt her. She had to pretend she'd forgotten it completely, that it had all meant nothing to her, a blip on the screen. If Connor dared bring up their past history, she'd make him change the subject. Or, she'd just leave. She hoped to heaven he wouldn't bring it up.

The elevator came to a stop at his floor, the very top, and she took a deep, steadying breath. She didn't know exactly how she was going to get through this, but she would.

When the doors of the private elevator finally opened, she found herself face to face with Connor. He smiled at her briefly, attractive lines she hadn't noticed before appearing at the corners of his eyes and bracketing his wide, sensual mouth. She looked away. She didn't want to notice how handsome he was, how very appealing she still found him. She didn't want her attraction to affect her tonight, though she knew her struggle to ignore those feelings was probably hopeless.

"Right on time," he remarked. He helped her out of her coat and hung it up, then politely stood aside while she stepped further out into the foyer of his vast loft apartment.

"I guess you didn't meet with much traffic tonight," he remarked.

"There was plenty of traffic. But I think my driver must have been flying fighter jets before he got work as a cabby."

The corner of Connor's mouth turned down in a small smile and Laurel gave herself a point for feigning enough composure to make a joke.

"Why don't you have a seat," Connor suggested. "And I'll get us something to drink." She followed him down a few steps, toward the seating area.

"Nothing for me, thank you," Laurel replied politely.

"Nothing at all? A glass of wine? Some coffee, or tea maybe? Take the chill off," he coaxed her.

"I'm fine, really," she insisted. "Actually, I'd like to just get started. I have another appointment in a little while."

Laurel hated to lie, but she couldn't help herself. She didn't want to prolong this get-together any more than was necessary, and wanted him to know he needn't treat her as if she was a dinner guest. She was here to discuss a business matter—an urgent business matter that would decide the fate of her brother's life, his family and her own. Not to sit and chat about the weather.

"Oh—of course." Connor seemed surprised for a moment. "Let's get started. I don't want to make you late for your date."

Had he put special emphasis on the last word? Or was that her imagination? He caught her eye and she quickly looked away. He'd seemed in good humor when he met her at the door but now was more sullen. If Laurel didn't know better, she'd say he was annoyed to hear she planned on cutting her visit short to keep some other engagement. How long did he expect this to take?

She felt a tight knot in her stomach as she chose a place on one of the burgundy leather couches. A large area rug in a kilm pattern set off the seating area. A mission-style rocker and leather wingback chair completed the arrangement. In what appeared to be an office area, a cluttered rolltop desk, with a notebook computer on top, stood nearby, along with some bookcases. The lighting was subdued, drawing her attention to the stunning river view, which was framed by a wall of long windows and wood-frame doors that led out to a courtyard. The place suited him, she thought, the atmosphere stylish and comfortable, and very sophisticated.

Connor took a seat across from her, in the reading chair. As he made himself comfortable, she secretly appraised his casual outfit of worn jeans and a black rolled-neck sweater. His cheeks were shadowed by a day's growth of beard and his thick hair was a little mussed. He looked different from his workday mode—but unfortunately, even more masculine and appealing.

She suddenly wondered how he'd managed to make it so long without some woman persuading him to the altar. But maybe in all the years they'd been out of touch, he had been married, and divorced. And maybe he was involved in a serious relationship right now. There was so much she didn't know about him anymore. She'd do well to remember that, Laurel admonished herself.

"Laurel, you said you wanted to talk some more about Phillip's situation. How can I help you?"

As she met Connor's steady gaze, his understanding expression was almost her undoing. So far, she had not been able to confide this monumental problem to anyone, and at times, she felt as if she might just explode. But it would hardly do to break down here, and cry, no matter how tempting Connor's strong shoulder looked to her right now.

"The situation is this," she began in as firm a voice as she could summon. "Phillip and I are unable to replace the missing funds. We don't have the money and simply can't raise it," she stated bluntly. "My father provided me with a trust fund, but I don't have access to it for at least two more years. And even if we sell the house on the Cape, we'll need to pay off a large loan at the time of sale. There won't be that much left…well, not enough anyway."

"Oh, yes…the house," Connor said thoughtfully. He rubbed his cheek with his hand. The mere mention of the place brought back a flood of memories for Laurel, and she guessed, for him, as well. But she refused to give recognition to the moment, though his penetrating stare seemed to demand it of her.

"There are other assets," she continued in a sharper, more businesslike tone. "But the math just doesn't work out in our favor."

"In Phillip's favor, you mean," he corrected her.

"This…problem affects many more people than Phillip," Laurel replied. "He has a wife, you know. And two children, a boy and a girl. They're still very young. They won't understand what's happened if he goes to jail."

She hadn't meant to talk about Phillip's children. It had just burst out. Nonetheless, it was all true and a serious consideration. But she could see that the information did not sit well with Connor. He looked down a moment before replying. A muscle twitched in his lean cheek as he seemed to struggle for control.

"I feel badly for Phillip's wife and children. I truly do," he assured her. "But if you've come here tonight to talk to me about how hard this situation is going to be on his wife and children, you've come to the wrong place. *Phillip* is the one who should have given them more thought, months ago. And given your welfare more consideration, I might add. But I sincerely doubt that your brother ever thinks much about anyone but himself," he added in a quieter tone.

The truth of Connor's words stung. Laurel could not argue with him. It seemed pointless to try to defend Phillip. Especially to Connor. Suddenly, the entire effort of coming here seemed futile and Laurel felt the impulse to simply get up and go home.

But she didn't. She couldn't. She was not only Phillip's sister, she was also here as his attorney. If they were ever going to get from A to B in this conversation, she had to figure out some angle around Connor's disdain for her brother.

"Phillip understands what he's done. He made an awful mistake, which he truly regrets. I don't think anyone can say that they've never made a mistake. Or a misjudgment. No one lives free of regrets. Not even you, Connor," she countered.

"Of course not," he answered quietly. The way he looked at her just then made her heart miss a beat. Was he thinking of their night together on the beach? Did he now count that episode as one of his more memorable mistakes? She felt the blood rush to her cheeks and she stared down at her hands, clasped in her lap.

"You've talked about Phillip and his family, but you've never mentioned yourself, Laurel," Connor observed. "How you'll be affected, I mean."

"I think we both know the answer," she replied grimly. "I'll be suspected of being an accomplice to Phillip's criminal activity. And even after I prove I'm innocent, my career in law will be ruined." She met his gaze, wondering suddenly if he thought she had been in on Phillip's scheme. "Or perhaps you think I was partners with Phillip in this mess?"

"No, never." He shook his head with a solemn expression. "Not you. Though I am amazed at how you can come here like this to plead his case, after what he's done to you."

"He's still my brother, no matter what he's done. He's all the family I have left."

"And you're still loyal and forgiving beyond what Phillip deserves," Connor replied, his tone tight with suppressed anger. "You haven't changed, Laurel," Connor murmured. "Still defending Phillip. Still helping him out of his messes."

"We do need your help," she replied honestly. "All of us. Isn't there something you could do? Some way to hide the missing funds until we can figure out a way to pay it back?"

He stared back at her, his forehead in deep furrows. He ran his hand through his hair and then abruptly stood up and paced across the room, toward the windows. "I might manage to do something, but with a gap this large, it would be tricky. I'd be taking an enormous risk," he admitted.

In his deep voice Laurel heard a mixture of sympathy and regret. She honestly believed that, despite everything, Connor wanted to help. But his hands were tied. What did Phillip think would happen here tonight? Connor would wave a magic wand and make this entire mess disappear—poof!—just like that? It had been a foolish, desperate hope on both their parts. She could see that now.

"Yes, I understand. Besides, why would you risk going to jail yourself to help Phillip?" she asked.

He stood looking out the window with his back turned toward her and she wasn't even sure that he'd heard her. Then, what seemed like a long time later, he turned and met her gaze.

"I'd do it for you," he said quietly. "Despite everything. You're the only reason I didn't go straight to the board with this information. Your brother would be sitting in jail by now if you weren't tangled up in this mess."

Again, that soft sympathetic look of his, melting her defenses. Why did he have to do that to her? She didn't want his sympathy. Especially not now. She pulled her gaze from his, mentally pushing him away.

"Is that supposed to make me feel better, Connor? It doesn't," she replied. Hearing him admit that he'd thought of her in that protective way actually did make her feel better—worlds better—though she'd never admit it to him now.

Laurel stood up. "I guess we've both said everything we have to say tonight. I'll be going now." She pushed herself to sound brisk and businesslike, but her voice sounded hollow and defeated, even to her own ears.

Connor walked toward her and stood in front of her, blocking her way. When he looked down at her, the only way she could describe his stare was hungry—hungry for the sight of her—as if this brief visit had not satisfied his need at all. The intuition made her heart race. She assured herself that she had to be imagining it.

"No, don't go yet. There still may be a way out of this for you and Phillip."

"Short of leaving the country, I really can't imagine what you mean," Laurel said.

"No, nothing like that," he promised her. "Here, sit down again. Are you sure I can't get you something to drink?"

Laurel shook her head. "I'm fine. Honestly." She noticed that Connor suddenly looked tense, as if whatever he was about to suggest was hard for him to talk about. Was it something illegal? No matter what he had said before—and what she had felt about that admission—she honestly didn't want him to compromise himself for her sake.

He took a seat at the other end of the couch, where she was seated. The couch seemed suddenly smaller—and he seemed too close for comfort. When he turned and looked at her, the intensity in his gaze made her heart skip a beat.

"Do you ever think about the past, Laurel? About us, I mean?"

Finally, the moment she dreaded. Connor confronting her, dredging up the past. It was almost a relief now that it had come. Still, she could hardly speak around the lump in her throat.

Of course she'd thought of him. For too long a time, he'd been in her thoughts every minute of every hour. Even after he'd broken her heart. Even during her marriage. Then somehow she'd willed herself to put those thoughts aside. Still, images of Connor, of what might have been, crept into her dreams and most secret fantasies. During the past few days, since the meeting at her office, she'd thought of him more than she'd ever admit.

But what good would it do now to dredge up the past? Laurel saw no point to it. Was he about to apologize for the shameless way he'd treated her? Even if he did, it was far too little too late to make a difference. Wasn't it?

Laurel took a deep breath and stared straight ahead when she spoke, not daring to be caught again in the dark warm depths of his gaze. "Was there ever an 'us,' Connor?" she asked bluntly. "I remember a friendship in our childhood. And then, some postscript on the beach at night that I guess you might call a sexual encounter. Youthful hormones running wild, and all that. A lot of heartfelt promises we should have known better wouldn't stand up to the light of day,'' she added, her bright, cynical tone barely hiding the pain of a wound reopened. ''But it's all ancient history to me, honestly. Just more water under the bridge.''

Stealing a quick glance at Connor, she found him rubbing the back of his neck with his hand, his beautiful face in a grim, almost pained expression. She had promised herself time and again that if they ever had this conversation, she wouldn't play the victim. She'd never let him see how much he'd hurt her. But obviously, her words had struck home and he still felt guilty.

''Even after hearing you describe it that way, I have to confess, I still don't believe the time we had together meant so little to you.'' Connor's voice was strained, his tone so low she strained to hear his reply. He rose abruptly to his feet. ''I won't believe it, Laurel,'' he admitted finally as he came to stand before her. ''Even if you had your doubts later. Even if you felt making love with me was wrong because of your commitment to Todd. I could understand that. But I know what I felt that night…and what you felt in my arms. And I'll never believe it was just a casual encounter for you. An easy thrill,'' he added, a cutting edge of anger to his tone. ''You're not now, and never will be, that type.''

Laurel sat dumbstruck at his impassioned confession. As if he was the injured party in all this! How dare he act as if she had somehow wronged him.

She'd encountered totally self-centered men before—
she'd even been foolish enough to marry one. But this
had to be the absolute limit! He'd totally humiliated
her, used her and tossed her aside. And now he expected some confession on her part of how important
that night was to her?

"How dare you!" Laurel stood up to face him.
"Don't presume you know me anymore, Connor. Believe me, you haven't a clue. And even if I did have
some special feelings for you that night—however re-
grettable they turned out to be—why should I give
you the satisfaction of admitting it now?"

"Because, dear Laurel," he said, gripping her
shoulders, "the truth can set you free. It can set us
both free—"

And before she had a moment to summon a reply,
or to pull away, Connor's firm hold on her shoulders
softened and his mouth came down on hers, the touch
of his lips bold and possessive. His mouth moving
over hers with hungry abandon.

Laurel struggled against the assault for a moment,
but she knew she had no chance to resist him—or to
control the craving of her own body for his touch. As
she relaxed in his embrace and felt him draw her
closer, her mouth softened under his and she couldn't
help but respond to his embrace.

For an instant, there was no past and no future—
just an ever-present "now" filled with Connor's kiss.
She felt no anger toward him, nor any pain from the
past. There was nothing but the sensation of his nearness, his strong arms encircling her, his firm lips
working their magic. A golden warmth suffused her
body and soul, as if a bank of clouds had suddenly
parted to reveal the brilliant sun. How had she lived

so long without that blissful heat and light in her life? Laurel wondered. How had she ever managed?

But as Connor's kiss deepened and his strong hands swept over her slim form, reality slowly set in. What was she doing, losing herself in this man's arms again? Hadn't she learned her lesson? Laurel abruptly pulled away and touched her hand to her lips. A wave of self-reproach washed over her.

"Laurel?" His voice was soft, tender. She felt him gently touch her hair, which had come loose under his exploring fingers. She stepped back, out of his reach, as she struggled to regain her composure.

"Well, you've proved your point. Just as you did the last time we were alone together. But I still don't see how it adds up to much," she added curtly, hoping to hurt him.

He stared at her, then dragged his hand through his thick dark hair. If she didn't know better, she would have said he felt just as shaken from their embrace as she did. He walked across the room and poured himself a drink from the decanter on a low console.

"I think I found out what I needed to know," he said finally. His small, satisfied smile unnerved her.

"Well, that makes one of us," Laurel replied, gripping hairpins in her teeth as she hurriedly put herself back in order. "Are you finished with this little stroll down memory lane? I am."

"Just one more thing," he said in a matter-of-fact tone. "No matter what you felt afterward—guilt, confusion, maybe you were even angry at me for turning your life upside down—but why didn't you ever answer my letter? It seemed so unlike you to ignore it."

"Your letter? What letter?" He looked genuinely

surprised. And distressed at her reply. Laurel's heart jumped against her ribs.

Was there a letter? God, how many times she'd wished and even prayed that Connor would call or write to offer some comforting word. She hadn't even expected any big apology. Just some explanation for his actions, no matter how meager. Just some clue that their time together had been more than a quick conquest for him. Had he really left her a letter? Did she dare believe him?

"The letter I left for you the morning after we were together. I put it under the front door of your house myself. There's no way that you wouldn't have received it."

Laurel moved away from him and took a deep, steadying breath. Though her foolish heart urged her to believe this wild tale, her rational side scolded her for once again playing into his hands like a silly schoolgirl. She had always known Connor was a man of many talents, but she'd never imagined such skill as an actor among them.

"I never got a letter from you," she said evenly. "Not the next morning. Not ever," she added in her most definite courtroom tone. "And I believe that there's a very good reason for that," she continued before he could interrupt. "I never found a letter because there was none, Connor."

She stared at him, her wide eyes meeting his dark, measuring gaze. Again, he looked shocked for a moment, and then as if he was about to launch into a full-fledged argument with her. But suddenly, he seemed to pull back within himself. His expression became blank, unreadable.

You dismissed his word and you've hurt him, her

heart said, explaining his reaction. Don't be stupid, her rational side argued back. If he's telling the truth, why doesn't he say anything now? Why doesn't he insist there was a letter, or tell you what was in it?

"If what you say is true, that would explain a great deal," he said quietly.

'You're doubting *me?*" Laurel replied with a hollow laugh. The irony of the moment would have made her laugh for hours—if she wasn't so blasted angry at him.

But she battled to control her temper. "I'm not the one here who's making up convenient stories tonight, Connor. Reinventing history. For heaven's sake, I never wanted to discuss any of this in the first place," she reminded him as she gathered her briefcase and prepared to go. "I think we've had enough stories for one night. If you'll excuse me?" she said curtly. Then she quickly turned her back on him as she headed for the front door.

"Run off in a huff if you like," Connor said calmly, "but I have a deal to offer you, a way out of the mess your brother created. Aren't you at least interested in hearing what I have to say?"

Laurel stopped and stood a moment at the steps to the foyer, considering his words. Oh, yes. He had some proposal to make, hadn't he? Isn't that the way the conversation had begun? She rubbed her forehead with her fingertips. This conversation had gotten entirely out of control. Wasn't that the first thing they taught you in law school, never lose control of the discourse, especially in a negotiation? She had the urge to keep walking right out the door. Then she stopped herself. She'd come this far. She might as well hear what he had to say.

"Okay, I'm listening," she said, turning to face him.

When she lifted her head to look at him, his solemn expression made her skin prickle with awareness. His entire body language made her uneasy. He took a few steps closer—smooth, definite steps, like a powerful, sleek animal moving in on its prey. He gazed down at her, his arms crossed over his broad chest, the fabric of his sweater pulled taut, outlining his wide shoulders and muscular arms.

"I'm willing to cover up the accounting discrepancies and repay the lost funds myself if certain conditions can be met," he stated.

"Yes?" Laurel's mouth went dry. What was he up to? Hadn't he said that his hands were tied, he had no way of helping her?

"The first is that Phillip resign immediately. He can plead poor health, or some such excuse. Since he's doing such a bad job, no one will ask many questions. I think you'd be the appropriate choice to take his place, at least until a permanent replacement can be found."

"All right, that can be accomplished easily enough," Laurel answered carefully. She had no need to check with her brother on this point. She knew Phillip was eager to leave the business. But what else did Connor want? And what would he be gaining from this rescue?

"What else?" Her stomach twisted in knots as she waited for the other shoe to drop.

"The second condition is that Phillip signs over his share of the house on Cape Cod to you. I assume that you now own it jointly?"

"Yes, since my father died," she told him, though

she hardly understood why the issue could be important to him in any way. "Is there anything else?" she asked slowly.

"Yes, just one more thing. The third condition is that you marry me." His tone was smooth and businesslike. He caught her gaze and held it, his own, steady and unflinching.

Laurel stood in shock, staring back at him. Her briefcase dropped from her hand and landed with a loud thump on the polished wooden floor, but she'd hardly noticed.

"Marry you? Are you mad?"

"I've never been saner in my life." He took a step toward her and Laurel actually felt her knees shake.

Was this some kind of cruel joke? His deadly serious expression told her that it was not.

"I don't understand...." Feeling dazed, she shook her head. She must have looked unsteady on her feet, for at that moment, Connor reached out to grasp her elbow.

"Laurel, are you okay? I'm sorry if I've shocked you. Perhaps you should come inside again and sit down. Let me get you some water," he said solicitously.

"I don't need any water, thank you," she replied curtly, shaking off his hold. She did feel dizzy, but she fought off the urge to lean on the strong arm he offered for support.

"Why?" she demanded finally. "Why in heaven's name do you think you want to marry me? The whole idea is just...insane, Connor."

Connor shrugged his broad shoulders, his sensuous mouth lifted in a small, private smile. "Because I know now I should have married you seven years ago.''

''That's ridiculous,'' she countered with a shake of her head.

''Oh, I don't know about that, Laurel. If I ever had any doubt, that kiss just convinced me otherwise—''

''That kiss proved nothing,'' she countered fiercely.

''Say what you will,'' he continued, unfazed by her denial. ''I think if I had asked you back then, you would have said yes.''

The brazen audacity of the man was astounding! Laurel felt an impulse to simply slap him across the face. Instead, she quickly picked up her briefcase and scooped up her overcoat from a nearby chair.

''You're so sure of yourself, aren't you?'' she asked as she turned to go. She stepped up to the private elevator and swung open the heavy door. ''We'll never know what I might have said way back when. But I do know that my answer tonight is an unequivocal no.''

As she stepped into the elevator and punched the button for the first floor, Connor held the door open. His large frame filled the space and made her feel suddenly cornered. ''I'll go down with you and see you into a cab.''

''That won't be necessary. Please don't bother,'' Laurel replied. She wanted to get away from him as fast as possible, and that message must have been conveyed in her polite reply since Connor quickly acquiesced.

''All right, if you say so.'' Still, he lingered in the doorway, making it impossible for her to go. ''I'm sure my proposal has taken you by surprise. You need some time alone, to think things through.''

''My feelings about this won't change, Connor. You're wasting your time to think otherwise,'' she promised him.

He stared at her for a long moment, enveloping her in a warm, dark gaze. She felt as if he had reached out and touched her, when, in fact, he remained motionless, an arm's length away.

Then he did reach out and touch her, lightly tracing the line of her cheek with his fingertips as he pushed aside a strand of her hair. ''Get home safely tonight,'' he said in a tender voice that, despite everything, still had the power to affect her. ''We'll talk again soon.''

She couldn't speak and simply nodded. He stepped back and the elevator's doors closed. When she reached the first floor, Laurel walked through the lobby in a daze. The doorman offered to hail her a cab, but she decided a walk in the brisk night air might clear her head.

The night had grown considerably colder while she'd been visiting Connor, and a frigid wind gusted down the narrow streets, tossing litter and soot in its wake. Heedless of the cold, Laurel walked along as if in a trance, her open coat flapping around her slim body. Her thoughts were scattered and confused as one question echoed in her mind, repeated again and again, in time with her heavy steps. *What was she going to do now?... What in the world was she going to do?*

When Laurel finally returned to her apartment on the Upper East Side, she practically crawled in the door, too exhausted to even hang up her coat. In the bedroom, her telephone answering machine was blinking furiously. The counter indicated five messages. She privately bet herself a million dollars that the messages were all from Phillip, wanting to know how the meeting had turned out. She hit the playback button and listened as she stripped off her clothes.

Phillip's anxious, irritated voice rattled on as Laurel went into the bathroom and ran the shower. She was too tired to call him back tonight. Besides, she wasn't sure what to tell him. She needed a little time to think this through.

The last message was from Connor, his deep, warm voice expressing concern. He was checking to see that she'd gotten home all right and wanted to wish her good night again. He also added that he hoped she'd give more thought to his proposal.

How could she think of anything else?

Finally, the messages were over and she stepped under the warm spray, wishing the water could wash away everything, inside and out—her worries, her memories…and desires.

As she scrubbed her smooth body with a washcloth, sensations of Connor's embrace returned unbidden. She remembered the way he'd held her and kissed her. She remembered the way she'd responded to him, and again reproached herself for giving in to him so easily. Well, maybe it was just an experiment, Laurel decided, and she could overlook that misstep just this once. Maybe some small part of her was curious, too—just as he had been.

For the record, she noted, the experiment had clearly been a success. The chemistry was still there, stronger than ever. Neither could have any doubt.

But was that any reason to propose marriage? A reason to try to seduce her perhaps. But *marry* her?

Not in this day and age.

And certainly not when a man like Connor could have his pick of just about any woman in New York City.

He claimed he was trying to rewrite history, to do what he should have done years ago. But she was hardly the same person she'd been years ago, so trusting and loving, abandoning herself in his arms. No, she was untrusting now. Disillusioned with romance. He'd done this to her, as much as her disappointing marriage to Todd.

Laurel slipped into bed and shut out the light. But her troubled thoughts wouldn't let her sleep. Had Connor really left her a letter, as he now claimed? If he had, why didn't she receive it? If there had been a letter, she would have given the world right now to know what it had said. Had he repeated his claim to love her, or had he doubted and denied those promises, expressing misgivings about what they had done?

Laurel didn't know why her eyes were suddenly filling with tears, but they were. She wiped them with the back of her hand. She didn't think she had any more tears left to shed over Connor Northrup. And she wouldn't let him make a fool of her again.

No, as much as she wanted to, she didn't believe him. That convenient fairy tale was part of his plan, she decided. A gambit to try to soften her hardened feelings toward him.

She rolled onto her side and punched up her pillow. As she tried to puzzle out his motives for offering her marriage, she could only come to one conclusion. It was his way of somehow getting even with her family. Although she'd never noticed any bitterness on his part over the difference in their wealth and status, that didn't mean it wasn't there. Maybe she just didn't want to see it.

Her parents had always treated Connor kindly, especially her father. But maybe, even in her father's generosity, Connor had felt condescended to, like the poor boy tossed some scraps from the noble lord's table. And she couldn't forget that his parents had worked for most of their lives as servants to her family. Phillip had always gone out of his way to send that message to Connor, Laurel knew only too well. Phillip had treated Connor like a second-class citizen while growing up. Connor had always seemed to rise above Phillip's insults. But it must have hurt him, deep down inside, and he was far too proud to let anyone know how much those barbs had wounded him.

So maybe now, forcing Charles Sutherland's daughter to marry him was some twisted way for Connor to finally get his revenge, Laurel reasoned. It was the same conclusion she'd come to time and again, whenever she tried to understand why he had seduced her on the beach the night of her engagement party, promising her the world as she lay lovingly in his arms. And then, he disappeared without a word. He'd just wanted the conquest—winning the girl who had always been out of reach. Getting back at her family for insults silently endured for years.

She had never thought of Connor as cruel—anything but. She still couldn't think of him that way. But maybe there was a dark side of him that she'd never wanted to see, Laurel speculated.

Still, what could you say about a man who would present a woman with a choice like this one? Marry a man who humiliated you and broke your heart—a man who has made it abundantly clear he can never love you. Or, watch your brother go to jail and his family go to ruin.

Feeling exhausted, Laurel drifted into a troubled sleep.

Four

―――

"Late night?" Laurel's secretary, Emily, greeted her as she followed Laurel into her office.

Laurel had overslept and then her cab downtown had hit a major traffic jam. She was feeling harried and out of sorts and it wasn't even nine-thirty.

"I didn't get much sleep," she admitted. "Then I missed the alarm."

She sat behind her desk and quickly opened an extra-large container of black coffee. It was steaming hot, and the aroma helped to revive her. She was so focused on getting her dose of caffeine that she barely noticed Emily's theatrical throat-clearing.

Finally, she looked up and met her gaze.

"Something you want to tell me, Em?" Laurel asked.

"You really must be out of it, Laurel, if you

haven't even noticed the flowers on your desk," Emily replied in dismay.

Laurel glanced around. Good heavens! There were flowers on her desk…. The huge arrangement looked like half a rain forest. Laurel gazed in fascination at the unusual combination of miniature orchids, orange bird-of-paradise, graceful sprays of bougainvillea and other exotic blossoms she could not name.

"There's the card," Emily prodded her.

"Yes, I see it," Laurel replied, though she made no move to open it.

"This one-stop garden show couldn't have something to do with your late night, could it?" Emily asked in a cheerful, gossipy tone.

"Well, actually…I'm afraid it does," Laurel admitted. "But not the way you probably think," she hastily added.

She took a quick, bracing breath, picked up the small envelope and slipped out the card. "Thinking of you—Connor," was all it said.

Well, she was definitely thinking of him, too. But hardly in such an amiable frame of mind.

Her intercom gave a shrill buzz and Laurel suddenly remembered that she'd never called Phillip back last night. "Could you get these out of here, please?" she asked, waving her hand at the flowers. "Put them in the reception area, or the cafeteria or something."

Emily picked up the flowers with a puzzled expression. "But, Laurel…"

"Please, just get them out of my sight," Laurel insisted. Without missing a beat, she hit the blinking button on her phone and picked up the receiver. She had barely greeted Phillip when he began his predictable ranting.

"Do you have any idea what you put me through last night?" he yelled into her ear. "I fell asleep sitting by the phone, waiting to hear from you. I was a complete wreck. I nearly told Liza everything."

Laurel had half a mind to tell Phillip that if his marriage was worth a plug nickel, he would have confided in Liza long ago. But she didn't want to provoke him any further than was necessary now.

"The meeting went longer than I thought," Laurel replied calmly.

"Well, that's a good sign," Phillip muttered. "Maybe, I mean… Well? What am I to think? *Is* it a good sign, Laurel? Is there any hope at all?"

Laurel had already carefully planned out what she'd say to her brother. Still, it was difficult for her to lie to him. "Connor made it clear that it would be difficult for him to help us. The losses are deep and hard to cover up. And there's his own reputation to consider."

"His reputation? Damn his reputation. My entire life is at stake. Who gives a damn about his reputation!"

At Phillip's vindictive blast, Laurel pulled the phone away from her ear.

"Now, Phillip, just calm down, will you?" she replied. "Connor also said that he might be willing to agree to some deal. But he wasn't specific," she lied. "He hasn't told me what his terms are yet."

"Probably wants us to sign over the entire firm to him," Phillip groused. "He always knew how to exploit a situation."

"Taking over the firm didn't seem to be his motive,

Phillip. We never discussed anything like that,'' she said honestly.

Despite her private misgivings about Connor, she bristled at Phillip's cutting remarks. She found herself either defending Connor, or silently seething at Phillip's unfair criticisms. If she thought Connor was so reprehensible, why was she so loyal to him? she had to ask herself.

Phillip's grating voice commanded her attention again and she tried to catch up to what he'd been saying.

''Well, when will he tell you what he has up his sleeve? I can't wait forever, you know.''

''Uh, soon. He'll tell us soon,'' she promised.

She knew the waiting was hard and felt badly for him. But she didn't dare confide the truth to Phillip. She wouldn't have a chance to think the situation over with a clear head if he got into the act. He'd be nagging her night and day to agree to the marriage, working on her sense of responsibility and making her feel guilty.

''Please do what you can to push him along,'' Phillip begged. ''I can't live like this, Laurel. I don't eat, I don't sleep and I'm just about jumping out of my skin.''

''Yes, I know it's hard, Phillip. But we'll have some answer soon,'' she assured him.

She heard a fumbling sound on the other end of the line. A sound that had become familiar, actually. Phillip, popping pills into his mouth and gulping down water.

''Phillip, what are you taking?'' she asked him bluntly.

''Just some tranquilizers. Very mild ones,'' he assured her. "They hardly do me any good. I ought to call the doctor and ask for something stronger."

Laurel tensed with alarm. Phillip was in a desperate and unstable state of mind. The idea that he might have access to anything stronger than aspirin filled her with dread. Sounding as calm as she could, she tried to dissuade him from taking any more medication.

"I don't think that's wise. Why don't you just get out of the office for a while? Take a long walk. Take the rest of the day off," she suggested.

"Yes, maybe I'll do that," he muttered. They reviewed a few incidental business matters and then Phillip hung up.

Laurel considered calling up her sister-in-law, Liza, and talking to her about Phillip. She didn't need to betray any confidences but thought Liza should know that Phillip needed extra care and attention right now since he was under a terrific amount of stress. When she called Phillip's home, the housekeeper told her that Mrs. Sutherland was out for the day and wasn't expected back until late in the evening.

Laurel next thought of calling Phillip's physician. She knew it was a breach of her brother's privacy, but she honestly thought his judgment couldn't be trusted now. He was unstable and might actually try to harm himself. But that call didn't yield any productive results either. Phillip's doctor was not available, and all Laurel could do was leave her name and number again, hoping he'd call back before the end of the day.

Laurel worked steadily, barely taking time to eat a light lunch at her desk. When Emily stood at her door, wearing her coat and hat, Laurel was surprised to lift her head and see that the January evening already looked dark and cold outside.

"I left that stack of letters in the red folder on your desk, to be signed," Emily told her. "And the first draft of the report is in the blue folder, for your review."

"Thank you," Laurel located the items on her desk, then smiled at Emily. "You have a good evening. See you tomorrow."

"Oh, I almost forgot..." Emily trotted back to her desk and then handed Laurel a pink message slip. "You had a call before. You were on the other line and had asked me not to interrupt you. He said he'd be there until at least six, if you wanted to call back."

As Laurel suspected, the message was from Connor. He wanted to have dinner with her. Well, she had no intention of calling him back.

She could feel Emily's curious stare boring down on her, but she put the message aside without explanation. They said good-night again and Emily left for the day.

Laurel continued working. When her phone buzzed, she hesitated to answer it, but a glance at the clock told her it was past seven. Past the hour when Connor might still be trying to contact her, she reasoned. Besides, maybe it was Phillip's doctor and she did want to speak to him.

Connor's voice greeted her, and Laurel was surprised. "You shouldn't be working so late," he said. "Tomorrow's another day, you know."

"Now, there's news," she replied dryly. Instead of annoying him, her smart remark made him laugh.

"Will you have dinner with me, Laurel? And don't

tell me you're not hungry. You must have worked up an appetite by now. I just want to talk, honestly.... I think I made a perfect mess of things last night.''

"Oh? Does this mean you're retracting your proposal?'' she asked curiously. She didn't know why, but her heart raced double time as she waited for his answer.

"Not at all,'' he replied adamantly. ''I just think I could have expressed myself in a...more persuasive way.''

"I think you expressed yourself very clearly, Connor. I think I understand you perfectly.''

"Have you given it any more thought?'' he asked quietly.

"I've thought about nothing else all day,'' she admitted. ''How could I?''

"And is your answer still the same?''

His voice sounded steady and deep. Yet, had she heard a slight tremor in his question? Laurel wondered. Or had she simply imagined it?

"I...I'm not sure,'' she confessed. ''I know it should be,'' she insisted. ''But there are other considerations. Other people involved,'' she added, thinking of Phillip and his family. ''But of course, you already know the way the deck is stacked in this game, Connor.''

She heard him take a long breath before he answered her.

"I do want to see you tonight, Laurel. I want to speak with you, face-to-face. Even for a few minutes... There are things I still need to explain,'' he said.

"No, there's nothing else to say,'' she replied. ''I

need to think about this more. At least overnight. I'll give you my answer tomorrow,'' she promised.

Then, without saying goodbye, she hung up the phone.

Laurel tried to continue working, but it was hopeless to try to concentrate. Finally, she gathered her things and left her office. On the way out, she decided to drop off a draft contract that Phillip needed to review. She left it in a folder with a sticky note on top in his secretary's in-box. His secretary was long gone for the night, and Phillip's office looked empty as well. Except for a thin shaft of light that filtered out from the direction of the private bathroom, she noticed.

Laurel didn't think much of the light and was about to head back toward the elevators. Then she decided to investigate. The least she could do, she reasoned, was shut off the light, which must have been left on by accident.

She walked through Phillip's darkened office, suddenly feeling gooseflesh break out on her skin. His desk was unusually neat, clear of the usual clutter of papers and file folders.

A white envelope rested against the bottom of a silver pen holder. Laurel stared down at it for an instant, just long enough to discern her name written in dark bold letters. She was about to reach for it, when a scraping sound from the bathroom broke into her consciousness.

She took a quick, startled breath, then rushed toward the bathroom. She pushed open the door. Just as she'd imagined in her worst fantasies, her brother lay sprawled across the floor, either asleep—or unconscious. She couldn't tell at first sight. The sharp scent of whiskey filled the air. His sweaty body reeked of it. She glanced down and saw an empty bottle of premium Irish whiskey in the corner of the room. Amber bottles with prescription labels were scattered on the sink counter.

"Good Lord," Laurel gasped. What had he done? She knelt and felt his neck for a pulse. Feeling it beat strong and steady, she sent up a silent thankful prayer.

Recalling what she'd learned in a first-aid class, she checked his eyes next. He didn't appear to be unconscious, just in a deep, drunken sleep. She loosened his collar, then pulled and pushed him upright so that he was seated leaning against the wall.

"Phillip?" she called to him. She gently slapped his cheek, which drew a groggy but brief response. She tried again, and when he didn't open his eyes, she wet a cloth with icy-cold water and pressed it to his head. "Phillip? It's Laurel, can you answer me?" she demanded.

He responded with an encouraging moan. "Come on, open your eyes," she coaxed as she applied a fresh dose of cold water.

"Leave me be," he muttered in a slurred tongue. Fumbling, he tried to push her away. "Go 'way." His eyes fluttered open for a moment and he stared at her. Then he sank down again. "Leave me," he groaned.

"Did you take any of those pills, Phillip?" When he didn't reply, she grabbed his shoulders and shook him. "Did you, Phillip? I have to know."

He moaned again and shook his head, "No. Just drunk." He turned his head to the wall and covered his face with his hands. "Wimped out. Story of my life…"

Laurel breathed a heartfelt sigh of relief. She slapped the wet cloth back on his forehead, then checked the bottles, just to be doubly sure he was telling the truth.

As she suspected, the bottles were a new prescription that had been filled today. A far stronger drug than he'd been taking, too. She wasn't a medical expert, but she suspected that an overdose of the stuff could have been tragic. Fortunately, the bottles all looked filled to the brim. She felt just about certain he was telling her the truth. Still, as she stared at him, she shuddered to think what might have happened. Dark images filled her mind and Laurel felt a frigid chill.

Poor Phillip. She knew his faults better than anyone. But she sympathized with him and wanted to help him. He was her brother, her closest living relative now that their parents were gone. It was her duty to help him, to protect him, any way she could. It was more than her duty, Laurel thought. She wanted to help him because she loved him.

Phillip groaned and tossed his head. He pulled the wet cloth off and tossed it on the floor. "God, I feel wretched," he grumbled. He gripped his stomach and made a face.

Laurel knelt beside him. "I think you need to see a doctor. I'll call an ambulance."

His sudden reaction lifted her spirits. He raised his head and peered at her with bloodshot eyes. Then he laughed out loud, right in her face. "I'm just drunk, dearie. No need to call out the militia. Just your average, garden-variety, totally inebriated sot. But you wouldn't know about such things, Laurel dear," he added as he fumbled to right himself. "You've led such a sheltered life."

Maybe she *had* led a sheltered life. She'd certainly seen people tipsy before. But never anyone who was this far gone.

"As long as it was only liquor, Phillip. You're absolutely sure?" she asked again as she leaned over to help him stand up.

"Scout's honor." He tried to make the appropriate hand signal and his fingers curled in confusion.

"All right, let's get you home. Lean on me, Phillip. We'll figure out something to tell Liza, I suppose."

"Liza—oh, yes. We'll come up with a good one for Liza," Phillip echoed, nodding. "You bet," he repeated agreeably. Laurel dropped him into a chair like a sock puppet, then found his coat and draped it over his shoulders. "You are a pal, Laurel. Did I ever tell you that?" Phillip insisted. "A genuine pal. Don't know what I'd do without you."

"Yes, yes, I'm sure," she said, humoring him. It was hard to get him up and moving again, but somehow she managed to haul him nearly all the way to the elevators.

Just as they approached, an elevator stopped on their floor and the doors opened. When two security guards exited and ran toward her, Laurel realized they must have spotted her struggling with Phillip on the close-circuit security TV. Both men had worked for the company for a long time and Laurel knew them by name.

After quickly determining that Phillip didn't need medical attention, the guards took over and helped him into the elevator. Downstairs, Laurel hailed a cab and they bundled Phillip inside. He muttered a bit during the ride, but otherwise sat with his eyes closed.

Laurel was thankful for the silence. She needed a few minutes to collect herself. She was still reeling inside, each time she thought about Phillip's narrow escape. She glanced over to see him sprawled out comfortably, sleeping like a baby.

He'll have a mighty sore head in the morning, but no permanent damage, she assured herself. At least this time, another voice warned.

When they arrived at Phillip's posh Park Avenue address, two doormen eagerly assisted her. With their help, she roused Phillip and got him up to his apartment. Luckily, the children were both asleep and Liza was out at the ballet with a friend, which made it easy to put Phillip swiftly to bed without endless explanations.

During the brief taxi ride to her own house, Laurel stared out at the passing city scenery as the car sped uptown. Tonight's events had put everything in sharp focus for her. Now she knew with indisputable clarity what she had to do. Phillip's life depended on it. The welfare of his wife and children hung in the balance. However impossible the idea of accepting Connor's proposal seemed to her, she simply had to grit her teeth and bear it. What other choice could she make, knowing what she knew now about Phillip's desperate state of mind?

She'd have to call Connor first thing tomorrow morning—or maybe even tonight, if it wasn't too late—and talk over the terms of their agreement. If he was going to make such an outrageous demand of her, then she should be able to spell out some terms of her own, she reasoned.

In her distracted state, Laurel paid the driver and strode toward her building without taking notice of the figure who stood in the shadows near her doorway. He moved toward her, blocking her path to the apartment entrance, and Laurel suddenly looked up in surprise and gave out a startled sound.

It was Connor. He'd been standing out in the cold, waiting for her. From the looks of his wind-tossed hair and ruddy cheeks, he'd been waiting a long time.

"What are you doing here?" she said.

"Now, there's a greeting to warm a man's heart," he replied wryly. "Waiting for you, of course."

Despite her abrupt comment, Laurel noticed that he still looked pleased to see her. And awfully handsome. She had the urge to smooth back his tousled hair and run her hand along his lean cheeks with their inviting five o'clock shadow. Why did he have to look so darned good all the time—like some smooth, seductive advertisement for masculine appeal? she silently ranted.

"Well, aren't you going to invite me up?" he asked, breaking into her thoughts.

"Uh—no," she replied in a definite tone. Seclusion with Connor in her apartment seemed like an awfully bad idea. Especially since she planned on accepting his proposal. He might get the entirely wrong idea, and Laurel knew in her heart that if he tried to kiss her again, she didn't have the energy—or the willpower—to resist him.

"I really need to speak with you, Laurel. I won't take very much of your time."

"I want to speak with you, too," she replied. She

noticed his thick eyebrows rise in a curious reaction. But he didn't ask her any questions. "There's a café around the corner. It's very casual and quiet. It'd be a good place to talk, I think," she suggested.

"Sounds perfect. Lead the way," he replied graciously.

It only took a few minutes to walk to the café and Laurel didn't feel the need to make small talk. As Connor fell into step beside her, she had a curious sensation. Once the feeling of walking beside him had been so natural, as much a part of her life as breathing. Now she was sharply aware of his nearness, his formidable masculine presence moving in time with her steps. And people who passed them on the street, seeing them together, would naturally think they were a couple. Though she had at one time longed for this very scene, it was so jarring, Laurel reflected, to think of herself and Connor that way.

Well, you'd better get used to it, another voice reminded her.

With such thoughts weighing heavily on her mind, Laurel entered the restaurant with him and followed the hostess to a quiet corner table. Instead of sitting across from her, as Laurel had expected, Connor took the seat closest to her. At the small table, their shoulders were almost brushing once they both sat down. Their waiter arrived immediately with menus, and they both passed on dinner, but each ordered a glass of wine.

Laurel felt suddenly and utterly exhausted. It must have showed on her face, because Connor didn't say anything at first. He simply reached over and took her hand in both of his own. "Didn't get much sleep last night, did you?"

"Not a wink," she admitted. Why did he pick the darnedest times to be so gentle and sweet to her? Didn't he know he was the enemy?

"I didn't either, if it's any compensation to you," he confessed. He looked down at her hand and gently stroked her fingers. "It's my fault. Our talk last night upset you. I meant what I said, but I think I could have put things…differently."

"If you're referring to the deal you offered me, Connor," she replied curtly, "sugarcoating it would have only made things worse. At least you were straightforward and made no pretense of there being any real feelings behind it."

It was hard to tell in the dim light, but Laurel could have sworn she saw him wince at her reply. His restless touch on her fingers stilled, though he didn't let go of her hand.

"So I suppose, if I attempted to restate things tonight—maybe to suggest that there *are* some real feelings behind my words—you'd see that as pretense. Just 'sugarcoating,' right?"

Her throat felt suddenly tight and all she could do was nod yes at him.

"Well, maybe I'm damned if I do…and damned if I don't. But I have to say what's on my mind. After you went through with your marriage to Parson, I tried like hell to forget you. It wasn't easy. I know now I never really succeeded," he admitted. "After we met at your office a few days ago, I wasn't able to get you out of my mind. And I know, God help me, you've never been out of my heart. I've been lying to myself, Laurel. All these years. Acting as if I didn't care…"

"Stop. Please stop," she insisted. She covered her

ears with her hands and squeezed her eyes shut. She couldn't stand to hear any more of this. It was everything she'd longed to hear him say. But sadly, much too late.

It was just too much—the trauma with Phillip, and now, having to face Connor, not as an adversary, like last night. But in this seductive atmosphere, while he sat holding her hand and gazing at her with such exquisite tenderness, saying words that should have been a healing balm for her battered heart.

But it was all an act. He believed she was about to refuse him. He didn't know she was going to agree. He'd stop at nothing to get his way.

The realization was like a dash of cold water in her face. And then, she did cry. She felt the tears slipping down her cheeks but refused to acknowledge them. And she knew she was crying for their lost love. Because no matter what he said now, she knew, in her heart, he didn't really love her.

Laurel swallowed hard and pulled her hand away from his. With a great effort, she collected herself. "You don't have to...put on this act, Connor.... I've changed my mind. I'll marry you."

His dark eyebrows drew together and he frowned at her. "I thought this afternoon you said—"

"Never mind what I said before," she replied sharply. "I'm giving you my answer right now. I'll do it."

"What changed your mind?" he persisted.

Did she dare tell him about the incident with Phillip? Once she would have gladly confided in him, but now she thought better of opening up to him that way. She couldn't show him her weakness. She simply didn't trust him anymore.

She shrugged. "I don't have much choice in the matter, do I? If it's what I have to do to solve this situation, I'll just bite the bullet and do it."

"You make the idea sound so...distasteful to you. Is it really that awful a fate?" he asked candidly.

He still looked thrown off stride, she noticed, and Laurel had the horrifying feeling that she'd gone too far. Maybe now he had second thoughts as well and was about to back out of the idea. She thought of Phillip and the disaster that would ensue if Connor didn't clean up this mess, as he'd promised.

"Don't ask me to lie to you, Connor. I think you know how I feel," Laurel replied, staring down at the table. Then she lifted her eyes and gazed at him. "Does your offer still hold?" she asked him point-blank.

Her heart nearly stopped when he looked away and didn't immediately answer her. He swirled the dark red wine in his glass, but didn't take a sip. Finally, he looked up again, his expression shuttered, unreadable.

"Yes, the offer still holds," he replied. The cold edge to his deep voice, which she hadn't heard before this moment, sent a chill up her spine.

Still, Laurel had no choice but to take a deep breath and continue. "Well, I agree to it then. On one condition," she added.

One eyebrow lifted in curiosity. "Which is?"

"After a year's time, if either of us wants a divorce, it will be granted by the other party, with no questions asked. Any money you lay out to repay the employee retirement fund will be returned to you," she promised, "if it takes me the rest of my life. And, I don't expect any personal gain from this arrangement," she assured him. "I'm willing to sign any type of pre-nuptial agreement you'd like."

"I hadn't even thought about a prenuptial agree-ment. If you marry me, you'd be my wife, in every sense of the word," he promised her. There was no mistaking his meaning in the gleam in his dark eyes. "I plan on taking care of you, Laurel. Whether you like that horribly old-fashioned idea or not," he taunted her. "And even if I do agree to this time-limit idea, I'd hardly let you leave me without knowing you were comfortably provided for."

"Paid well for my services, you mean?" she said.

His eyes narrowed and his fine lips tightened as she watched him push back an angry retort. "Don't worry, I'll make sure I get my money's worth," he replied, matching her tone. He watched her recoil at his words, and his lips lifted in a small, smug smile. "Wasn't that what you wanted me to say? After all, you've clearly cast me as the villain here. It doesn't have to be that way, you know," he added in a softer voice.

But it did. He didn't understand. She couldn't man-age to do this otherwise.

"So we're agreed on the terms?" she replied.

"All right. If that's the way you want it, I'll agree. But I insist on the appearance of a real marriage. For one thing, if it looks like anything less, people might get suspicious and we'll both be in hot water. You understand what I mean, don't you?"

"Yes, I understand." She took a deep breath and nodded.

He laughed, a deep, quiet rumble that was remark-ably sexy, Laurel had to secretly admit. "You needn't act as if you're being sentenced to a jail term, Laurel.

If anything, marrying me will save you from that fate.''

He was right. She was saved from a prison with bars—if it had ever come to that—only to face a far worse form of torture. To live with Connor as his wife, knowing it was not the union of loving hearts she'd once dreamed of, but only his way of living out some vengeful fantasy....

She felt suddenly sick to her stomach, perhaps at the realization of what she'd just agreed to.

''Are we quite done here?'' she asked abruptly.

''No,'' he shook his head, his gaze fixing on hers. ''We're not. You're not getting off quite so easily tonight, Laurel. As far as I'm concerned, the clock starts running right now....''

She knew from the gleam in his eye that he was about to kiss her. Her first impulse was to jump up and leave the restaurant as fast as her feet could carry her. But she sat motionless, unable to break her gaze from his, unable to even take a breath.

He leaned toward her, swiftly closing the small space between them, then reached out and cupped her cheek with his hand, holding her head firmly so that she couldn't turn away. With his mouth close to hers, he stared directly in her eyes. ''You're beautiful, Laurel. Even more so than years ago, if that's possible. Think whatever you want of me and my motives, but I promise, you won't be sorry you agreed to be my wife.''

Then his mouth met hers, softly at first, not tentative in any way, but with a sense of restrained power, as he savored the sensation of his lips on her own. Laurel tried her best not to respond, willing herself to remain unresponsive until the assault was over.

Yet, slowly but surely, his lips worked their seductive magic and she felt her resistance burn away like early-morning fog in the heat of the rising sun. Her hand that had been resting on his shoulder, pushing him back, relaxed against the soft fabric of his jacket and the firm muscles underneath. His kiss deepened and her head dropped back under the pressure of his mouth. Her hand moved higher, curling around his strong neck, her fingertips weaving into the thick dark hair at the back of his head.

As she relaxed in his embrace, his strong arms encircled her, one arm around her shoulders, the other resting at her slim waist. Her lips parted and she felt his hot, probing tongue moving against her own, circling and thrusting, coaxing her to an even fuller, franker expression of desire.

The way he kissed her left no doubt in Laurel's mind as to their future together as man and wife. Beneath all the hurt feelings, all the anger and dismay at this arrangement, Connor knew only too well that he would always hold a trump card in his favor. Their chemistry simmered on, as powerful as ever, an ever-burning flame that could never be satisfied.

As one part of her mind urged her to break free, another urged her to pull him closer, to match and answer the tempo of his thrusting tongue, to tease and tantalize him at the same feverish pace he now kissed her.

As Laurel felt her self-control slip away, it was Connor who suddenly and surprisingly broke away. Her eyes flew open to find him looking as stunned and unraveled as she felt.

''One more stipulation that just came to mind,'' he

murmured in a husky tone. "No long engagement. I want to be married by next week."

As he waited for her response, he dabbed at his mouth with a cocktail napkin, wiping away her lipstick. Laurel found the gesture inexplicably intimate—and exciting. She lost her train of thought and had to look away.

"Next week? That's impossible." she replied.

"Of course it's not," he argued. "I'll pick you up at your office around noon. We can look in Cartier first for the rings," he said. "Or maybe you'd like to be surprised. Do you know your ring size?" he asked, looking for all the world like a genuine, love-struck fiancé.

"You said you didn't want to attract suspicion, Connor. Don't you think a week is rather sudden?"

"Not when people hear that we knew each other way back when," he replied. "And I doubt any man who takes one look at you would wonder at my rush for an instant."

"Connor, be serious." She tried to ignore his outrageous compliment, but felt herself blushing all the same. "I wasn't thinking of a large party. Just Phillip and his wife, and a few friends. But it takes time to make arrangements."

"All right, I'll give you two weeks, then. But that's my absolute deadline," he said sternly. "In fact, why don't you leave everything to me? I'll name the place and time, and all you have to is show up…and say, 'I do,' a few times," he added with a sly smile.

He'd always been the take-charge type, but she'd never imagined he'd be taking charge of their wedding arrangements. Laurel wasn't used to handing over control so easily. But she decided to take Connor up on his offer. After all, it wasn't a real wedding—and it was all his idea anyway. It might even be upsetting to plan the affair, she realized.

"That sounds fine to me," she said. "In the meantime, I'll practice my lines." She pushed her chair back from the table and rose to go. He began to get up as well, but she stilled him with a firm touch on his shoulder.

"Don't bother, I can find my way home by myself. I'd prefer to, actually."

His expression darkened, and for a moment she thought he was about to argue with her. Then he dipped his head, nodding in assent. "As you prefer then... And sweet dreams, sweetheart," he added in a teasing whisper. "I know what I'll be dreaming of."

His sensuous mouth twisted in a tantalizing grin and Laurel felt a wave of heat wash over her body in response. She left without saying goodbye, and as she turned and walked away from the table, his low, sexy laugh followed her.

Five

Just as Connor had predicted, no one questioned their whirlwind courtship and marriage plans. Everyone seemed to think it was quite romantic, which was salt on the wound, as far as Laurel was concerned.

Not even Phillip knew the entire truth. Connor had made her promise not to tell him. So instead of confiding the deal she'd made to save him and the firm, she had to endure Phillip's smug, self-congratulatory attitude. When she told him that she and Connor were getting married, and that out of love for her, Connor had agreed to cover up the accounting discrepancies and repay the lost funds, instead of falling to his knees in gratitude—as she would have done, most probably—Phillip could not stop patting himself on the back, acting as if he had masterminded the entire solution.

Laurel ignored him and quickly changed the subject. She was ultimately grateful that the wedding was going to happen quickly. She didn't like all the attention she received as a bride-to-be and felt dishonest accepting everyone's well-wishes, and feigning an eager, joyful attitude.

Connor had no trouble, it seemed, acting out the role of her adoring fiancé and missed no chance to embrace her and even kiss her when they were in public. But while his ardent lovemaking continued in private as well, surprisingly he always stopped before things went beyond heated kisses and caresses.

During the first week of their engagement, Laurel continually expected him to make some demand upon her about starting an intimate relationship before their marriage. But the evenings they spent together ended with Connor escorting her to her door. When he politely declined her invitations to come in for coffee, Laurel knew she should have felt relieved…but instead, felt vaguely disappointed. It was a feeling she didn't like—and would never have dared admit. And she didn't dare question him about it either.

About a week before the wedding, Connor called to say that he needed to be out of town on business up until the very day of the ceremony. He'd be hopping through the major cities of Japan and also visiting Hong Kong. His schedule would be very hectic, but he would try to call, he promised. Laurel did her best to sound cool and nonchalant, but when she hung up, she felt suddenly panic-stricken. Was this all part of some dark, demonic plan? Had he set her up just to leave her at the altar and publicly humiliate her?

Her suspicions were shocking. She had to wonder how her notion of Connor had come so far, and thought back to the golden days when she'd admired him and trusted him implicitly. Trusted him with her life, in fact, in so many dangerous situations they'd gotten mixed up with as kids. Well, she was, in a sense, putting her life in his hands again, now, wasn't she? And feeling not so nearly sure of the outcome.

Laurel knew that despite her grave fears, there was nothing to do but carry on and play the role of the happy bride. When her wedding day arrived, Laurel had not heard from Connor for almost a week. A classic-style Rolls-Royce Connor had hired for the occasion carried her to the Saint Regis Hotel, where she met her brother and his wife and children. Their guests were starting to assemble in the small, elegant room Connor had reserved. He'd seen to every detail—from the abundant flower arrangements, to a string quartet. A distinguished-looking judge stood ready to hear their vows.

While the guests sipped champagne—and checked their watches, she noticed—Laurel waited in a small side room. The bride room, a hotel employee who was assisting in the affair had called it.

"Does it have a secret door for hasty exits?" Laurel quipped.

"Now what's that supposed to mean?" Phillip said sharply. Liza soothed him with a gentle touch on his sleeve. But the truth was, Phillip was acting more anxious than Laurel. Every five minutes, he pulled out his cell phone and dialed both Connor's home and office numbers.

To Laurel's thinking, Connor would either show up—or he wouldn't. Maybe she deserved to be left standing at the altar. She wasn't very proud of her reasons to marry him. It would be an embarrassment, surely, but secretly, a great relief. Hadn't she been praying for some miracle to save her from this marriage?

Still, some quiet, utterly honest voice inside her insisted that she wouldn't be relieved at all if Connor stood her up today—she'd be desperately disappointed. Heartbroken, even worse than the last time.

Laurel felt a hand on her shoulder. "Laurel, are you all right?" Liza, a sleek, dark-haired beauty looked at her with concern.

"I'm fine—just need some air, I think." Laurel rose from her seat and stepped out of the room.

She lifted her head—and saw him. He stood talking with the judge who would marry them, his dark head bowed, his thick hair freshly cut and smoothed back, emphasizing the strong lines of his face. His black tuxedo made him look even taller and made his physique appear even more impressive, she noticed. He looked altogether too handsome.

Her relief at his arrival was quickly replaced by another feeling—a feeling of being overwhelmed at the realization that this devastatingly attractive man would soon be her husband.

Laurel slipped back into the small room where Liza remained waiting. "Connor's here," she said calmly, then proceeded to freshen her appearance, though her hand trembled as she tried to apply some more lipstick.

She'd chosen a simple silk dress for the occasion. The fabric was champagne-colored and the lines form fitting and quite elegant. The long narrow skirt of the floor-length dress had a back slit that discreetly showed off her slim legs to advantage. The dress was sleeveless and fit closely at the low neckline and bodice.

Her hair had been swept up in something considerably more glamorous-looking than her usual style. She'd also added a small jeweled headpiece with a short veil. The only jewelry she'd chosen for the occasion were diamond stud earrings and the beautiful blue sapphire and diamond engagement ring she'd picked out with Connor. She gazed down at the ring as the guests took their seats and the music indicated the ceremony was about to start.

Laurel wasn't used to men buying her extravagant gifts. She wasn't used to anyone buying her gifts, for that matter, large or small. The day they'd met to choose the rings, Connor's desire to please her was nearly overwhelming. Laurel had to keep reminding herself that he was just playing his role. And of course, a man in his position couldn't have his wife wearing a skimpy engagement ring. If anything, he felt guilty about forcing her into this sham arrangement and was trying to soothe his conscience by spending money on her, she'd told herself. Still, when he'd finally slipped the ring on her finger, his expression had seemed so full of emotion, she'd almost believed he *did* have real feelings for her.

Phillip appeared and he walked with her up the short aisle. She was painfully aware of Connor waiting for her at the other end, but she could barely raise her head to meet his gaze. Finally, as Phillip retreated, she did.

He looked terribly solemn. She tried to read some clue to his thoughts in his dark eyes, but she couldn't. He took her hand, as the judge instructed, and quietly repeated his vows. His voice sounded steady and sincere, she noticed. When it was her turn, she heard her voice tremble.

They exchanged gold bands and the judge told Connor, "You may kiss the bride." When Connor leaned toward her, she moved willingly into his arms. She closed her eyes and felt the warm pressure of his mouth on her own. She didn't know why she suddenly felt like crying, but she thought that she just might. She felt relieved that the ordeal was finally over, of course. And relieved that Connor had arrived after all.

More than that, as she felt Connor possessively grip her waist, pulling her even closer, she felt a deep, soul-satisfying sense of belonging. As if she'd finally arrived at the place where she was meant to be. It was crazy, she knew. She was just getting swept away in the romantic fantasy of the wedding. But for the briefest moment, Laurel surrendered herself to the fantasy.

When they finally parted, Connor's hold lingered as he stood beaming at her—and reality once again moved in. "You won't be sorry you married me," he whispered.

Laurel turned her head away. "Just keep your end of the deal, Connor, and I'll keep mine," she whispered back.

Connor's fine mouth seemed to twist in a smirk at her retort. But looking as sure of himself as any new husband, he possessively gripped her arm and led her into the crowd of well-wishers. Some had already moved into an adjoining room, where a sumptuous array of gourmet foods was about to be served, along with vintage champagne and fine wines.

The party passed quickly and soon it was time for the bride and groom to depart. Laurel and Connor had decided that since her firm was in such disarray they would forgo a honeymoon trip. It was just as well for Laurel. She didn't like the idea of being secluded with Connor any more than was absolutely necessary.

They had also agreed that after the wedding she would move into Connor's large loft. She'd already moved in some of her clothes and possessions and fully expected to spend their wedding night there. But when they finally left the party together, Connor surprised her by hitting the uppermost button in the elevator and not L for Lobby.

"I booked the penthouse suite for the weekend," he explained. "I didn't want you to feel deprived of a honeymoon, Laurel."

The lustful gleam in his gaze mesmerized her. And terrified her.

Laurel's first impulse was to strike the red Emergency Stop button. But she tried to control her rising panic. After all, she knew all along that they would be living together as man and wife, in every sense of the word.

Still, the change in plans had pulled the rug out from under her. "But...why stay here? I thought we were going back to your place after the wedding."

"Too many distractions." His serious expression made her swallow hard.

"But...I don't even have a change of clothes."

He moved closer and rested his hand at the back of her neck. His strong fingers massaged the tense muscles at her nape. "You don't need any clothes. We're newlyweds, remember?"

"Connor—" She rested her hand flat against his broad chest. To keep him at a safe distance before he began making love to her in the elevator, she thought.

Yet, once she touched him, felt the heat of his skin through the thin white fabric, and felt his heart beating steadily beneath her palm, she forgot what she wanted to say. She ran her tongue over her dry lips in an unconsciously sexy gesture—one which was not lost on her husband, who watched her every move like a hungry tiger.

"Did you miss me while I was away?" he asked. With one arm wrapped around her slim waist, he pulled her very close, so close that she had no doubt about the extent of his desire for her. "I missed you," he whispered, leaning over to press his cheek to hers. Her senses were suddenly flooded with the warmth of his nearness, the spicy scent of his cologne mingled with the subtle but even more alluring scent of his warm skin. "It seemed like forever, waiting to see you again. I had a hell of a job trying to get back in time."

Despite herself, Laurel found his confession working on her, softening her heart and causing her bowstring-taut body to relax in his strong embrace.

"I nearly thought you were going to stand me up," she admitted.

He laughed and the deep sound warmed her. "Good. I'm glad I put a scare into you. Maybe that will make you appreciate me more.... But if that doesn't work, I have some other ideas to try tonight."

Although she tried not to give him the satisfaction of showing her response, his husky murmur stirred Laurel's senses and ignited her desire. For the past two weeks, she had forced herself to put aside thoughts of making love with Connor again, and had forced herself not to think about the last time. But here it was—their honeymoon night and the inevitable moment had arrived.

Before Laurel had much more time to think about it, they were at the door of their suite and Connor was fitting the key into the lock. He opened the door, but when Laurel tried to enter, he stopped her with a heavy hand on her bare shoulder. "Not so fast, dear. Isn't it customary for the groom to carry the bride over the threshold?"

"Don't be silly," Laurel insisted. She hated mocking the wedding rituals, which would have otherwise been carried out in the spirit of true love. Pretending this was a real marriage—that there was some genuine romantic feeling between them—was upsetting to her.

Couldn't he see that? Or did he say such things just to tease her?

"Uh-uh, I insist," he replied in a gentle but firm tone. And before Laurel could protest further, she found herself swept up in Connor's strong embrace. Having no choice, she submitted to him, and tried to show no reaction to his sexy, satisfied grin.

"Well, here we are—the honeymoon suite," Connor announced. He swung her around so she could take in the full view. Her annoyance at being carried around like so much baggage quickly faded as she gazed around their elegant and luxurious surroundings.

The suite consisted of a large living room with several Victorian-style satin love seats and armchairs arranged in front of a fireplace with a carved, white marble mantel. The pale marble floors were covered by thick Oriental carpets in floral patterns. Beyond the living room and dining area, Laurel could see a large bedroom, dominated by a high, wide bed. Another door led to a small kitchen. Everywhere she looked, the beautiful decor had been enhanced by magnificent bouquets of flowers and clusters of vanilla-white candles, their flickering, golden flames providing the only light.

The sumptuously decorated rooms were a perfect haven for two lovers to celebrate their union—a secret world where a man and woman could explore their passions to the fullest—and lose themselves in each other. At the French doors that led out to the balcony, a small table was set for two with sparkling crystal and elegant china.

Laurel knew without question that eating dinner right now was the last thing on Connor's mind.

"What do you think?" he asked bluntly, meeting her gaze.

What could she think? Any other woman would be touched, seeing how her new husband had gone to great expense and trouble to set the stage for their wedding night. But Laurel knew that for Connor, it really was just a stage—and she and he were merely actors playing their parts.

Laurel gazed into his questioning eyes briefly, then looked away. She was suddenly so conscious of his nearness, the feeling of his heavy muscles under her hand as she clung to his shoulders, the beard-roughened texture as his cheek brushed her own skin....

"I think...you need to put me down," she said finally.

"All right," Connor agreed, still watching her. She could see he was disappointed that she'd expressed no reaction to the room but that he was trying not to show it. As he set her down, one arm continued to circle her waist so that her lower body slid provocatively against his as her feet swung down to the floor.

As she finally stood again, he continued to hold her tight, his arms looped around her back. She pressed her palms against his chest and looked up at him to find his face coming closer, his expression as serious and intent as she'd ever seen it.

"I need to kiss you. I mean…really kiss you," he murmured. His low, husky tone set Laurel's nerve endings on super alert, and even before his mouth came down hard on her own, she felt an intense wave of heat course through her body. She had known for two weeks that this moment would come. She had spent hours, alone in her bed, considering how she would react, what she would say and do. But now that it was a reality, Laurel couldn't think. Couldn't speak.

The powerful expression of Connor's desire swept over her, pulling her along, like a fierce, irresistible tide. As Connor's tongue plundered her mouth, Laurel released a soft answering moan that seemed to encourage him even more. She felt his strong hands sweeping up and down her back, cupping her bottom and then up and under the edge of her thin, silk dress to stroke the bare skin on her back. His long, deep kisses ignited her secret desire for him and overruled any soft, distant whispers of resistance or dissent.

Yes, they were married and she had agreed to a marriage that was real in every way. But more than that, in one stark, blinding moment, Laurel faced the truth—she wanted to make love to him as much as he wanted her.

As their lips clung together, her hands moved over

his broad chest, and one by one unfastened the buttons of his shirt. He had already removed his tie and Laurel slipped her hand inside his shirt easily, stroking his skin and feeling the texture of the thick dark hair on his chest.

Connor groaned with deep satisfaction as her lips followed the teasing trail of her fingers. She felt his hands sweep up from her waist to cup both her breasts, tantalizing the sensitive tips to rigid points with his broad thumbs. Laurel's head lolled back as she gasped with pleasure. A molten river of heat coursed through her and her legs felt suddenly, but oh so pleasantly, weak. Connor's head dipped forward and his mouth covered the tip of each breast, delicately tasting and teasing through the thin silk. Giving herself over to the magnificent sensations, Laurel clung to his shoulders for support.

She had never felt this way in any other man's arms—and never would, Laurel thought hazily. How she had longed to have that experience again, to make love to Connor even one more time in her life. Even if it was for all the wrong reasons.

"I never wanted any woman more than I want you right now, Laurel," he told her quietly, "but I'd never force you to make love to me. Ever," he added solemnly. "So tell me right now if this isn't what you want."

Laurel couldn't speak and merely nodded, her face buried in his shoulder. Then she suddenly felt him move away and he lifted her chin with his fingertips so that she could not avoid looking straight into his eyes.

Laurel stared up at him, her mouth felt cottony dry.

Did she have to admit her desire to him? Wasn't that asking too much?

"But we agreed...how it would be," she whispered back in a faltering tone.

"To hell with the agreement," he answered brusquely. "Just tell me what you *honestly* want," he demanded, his gaze locked to her own. Was that really a flicker of vulnerability she'd spotted in his eyes? Or merely the reflection of candlelight?

"Well?" he urged her to answer, his grip tightening imperceptibly.

"Yes," she finally whispered. She stared back at him, and then away.

"Yes...what?" he prodded.

"Yes...I want you...I want to...to go to bed with you," she finally admitted. "Is that blunt enough for you?"

"Perfectly." He blinked. He seemed relieved by her answer...but not exactly pleased, she noticed. As if he had heard what he'd *needed* to hear, but not quite what he'd wanted.

As his face moved toward hers again, Laurel thought she saw an expression of regret, or perhaps resignation. But it was quickly replaced by one of intense desire. His lips moved down to cover hers again and, like a match dropped into a tinderbox, their passion ignited, exploded, white-hot and all-consuming.

In some foggy distant part of her mind, Laurel became aware that they had moved together as they kissed into the bedroom. They continued to kiss and caress each other, their tongues merged in a hot, wet dance of desire. Laurel felt an ache of longing within, painful and intense—a deep hunger that could only be satisfied by a complete union with the man who now held her so tightly in his embrace. As she felt Connor ease her down on to the bed, she heard herself sigh—a deep sigh of surrender…and satisfaction. She felt Connor's kiss deepen and heard his answering groan of bliss. Then she felt his strong hands sweep over her body, first in her hair, then moving down her slim form, leaving a pile of silk in their wake as he efficiently stripped off her wedding gown. He raised his head for a moment to appraise her and Laurel held her breath. Although she knew very well that Connor liked her looks—had even told her several times that he thought her beautiful—she still felt vulnerable to his judgment in this unclothed state. Especially after all the years they'd been apart. But the expression of awe on his face and the pure, unadulterated desire in his gaze quelled her every fear.

"You're so beautiful, Laurel," he said huskily as his mouth dropped to find hers again. "I hardly feel I have the right to hold you like this. But I sure as hell can't stop myself now."

His appreciative words had touched her. His compliments meant a lot to her, even if he really didn't love her, Laurel realized. She didn't know what to say and merely shifted her body, holding him closer, entwining her long legs with his.

"Don't you dare stop now," she replied finally, whispering into his ear. Her throaty tone held a hint of laughter and she felt Connor's smile as he pressed his face against her neck. She felt the air suddenly cool on her skin, then Connor's warm mouth pressed to the sensitive skin at the top of her breasts, exposed by the plunging neckline of the cream-colored lace bodysuit she'd worn under her dress. He murmured with delight as his warm mouth moved lower, first teasing one taut nipple through the lace and then the other. Laurel felt a thrilling shock of pleasure coursing through her limbs; she sighed and dug her hands into his thick hair. His large hands moved lower, gliding over her waist and hips, then finding the tops of her lace-edged stockings. He smoothed them from her legs, his fingertips caressing her thighs, building the heat even higher in her womanly core. Laurel's hands moved beneath his shirt, caressing his muscular back and hard torso. His body had changed little in the years that had passed since they'd last made love. If anything, he'd become even more desirable to her, she realized.

She secretly reveled in rediscovering his body, and sighed as she felt the thick mat of crisp dark hair on his chest. She swiftly undid the buttons on his shirt and pressed her face against his chest. His hands worked a special magic all over her body, molding, exploring, thrilling her beyond her wildest fantasy. She covered his hard chest with kisses, finding his flat male nipple and bathing it with her tongue, feeling his body tremble with pleasure and excitement against her. Her hands glided lovingly over his flat, taut stomach and down to cup his male hardness through the thin fabric of his pants. He groaned in the back of his throat, a deep thrilling sound—and Laurel felt emboldened by his response and the sensual power she seemed to have over him. She suddenly wanted so very much to please him, to take him to the very heights of passion, just as it once was between them. She'd never responded to any man the way she responded to Connor. She'd never felt as excited, or as desirable—or as uninhibited. No matter what the context of their lovemaking tonight—and all during their future marriage—when she was in Connor's arms, Laurel knew that in bed at least, they were a perfect match. He was the one man who could take her beyond the limits of her wildest fantasies—and secretly she knew, that she could do the same for him.

As Laurel struggled to unfasten Connor's belt with one hand, he suddenly sat up and quickly stripped off his shirt and trousers. He gazed deeply into her eyes as he moved back to lay beside her. Wordlessly, she opened her arms to him and moments later felt his beautiful body covering her. Their lips met once more and, lost in a swirling whirlpool of sensations, Laurel was only vaguely aware as her bodysuit was removed and Connor's caressing fingers discovered her feminine core. His rhythmic touch was so perfect, so pleasurable, Laurel could barely stand it.

"I want this to be perfect for you," he whispered as she arched her body toward his hand.

"It already is, Connor," she managed to reply between deep sighs of excitement. Just when Laurel thought she couldn't stand another second of his expert, tantalizing touch, she felt him move over her and slipped her legs around his hips. She felt him move inside of her, slowly at first and her arms tightened around him as the sweet, shocks of pleasure pierced her limbs. They moved together in a perfect, ageless rhythm and Laurel buried her face against his strong shoulder. As their passion climbed higher and higher, the sensation of their joining was so intense, so powerful, so satisfying, she wished their sensual dance would never end. But soon, she felt rocked by an explosion of ecstasy that seemed to set fire to every nerve ending in her body. She clung to Connor as her body trembled again and again. He moved powerfully within her, to push her even higher. Finally, she felt his body shake and grow taut as he reached his own peak, then heard his deep groan of satisfaction as he dropped down next to her. He covered her face with soft kisses as he pulled her close, cradling her in a warm, possessive embrace.

Laurel dozed with her head resting on Connor's chest. His eyes were closed and his deep breathing would have made her think he'd fallen asleep, except for his hand which continued to softly stroke her hair. "It's unbelievably wonderful to make love with you," he said softly. "Even better than the last time—though I didn't think that could be possible."

Laurel agreed totally but felt too shy to admit it. She merely murmured and nodded her head as her hand wandered appreciatively over his chest. "And the best thing about it is we don't have to wait seven years to do it again," he added as if he'd just realized the fact.

Laurel laughed lightly. "Good point."

"Actually, now that I think about it," he said softly, "we don't have to wait at all."

She felt the evidence of his continued desire and felt her own body stirring again in response. Instead of answering him with words, Laurel replied with her own loving touch, telling him with her boldly caressing hands and mouth that she didn't want to wait one more instant than was absolutely necessary to feel him inside of her again.

As Connor slowly came to consciousness, he felt the soft warmth of Laurel's body intimately entwined with his own, her silky hair splayed across his chest, her smooth cheek resting in the crook of his shoulder as she slept in naked splendor beside him.

His immediate impulse was to pull her even closer, to tighten his possessive embrace. But he didn't move a muscle; he knew once she woke, her rational, conscious mind would again take control and she would pull away from him, both physically and emotionally. Maybe she'd even regret that she'd fallen asleep in his arms. Maybe she'd even regret that she'd made love with him with such lack of inhibition, such abandon.

Unable to deny himself just one light touch, Connor gently ran his fingertips across a tempting golden strand of her hair. Could a woman really disdain a man, as Laurel seemed to disdain him—and then make love to him with such passion, such hunger? Maybe some women could, he considered. But not Laurel. Not *his* Laurel. She wasn't made that way, not back when he knew her—not now.

He'd been worried about their wedding night. He'd wanted her so very much and had honestly feared pressuring her into bed. If she had refused him, he wasn't sure what he would have done. A long, lonely walk around the city on a cold winter's night—his honeymoon night—certainly would have been one option. He knew he couldn't have made love to her if she'd expressed the least hesitation, no matter what they'd agreed upon. He'd never want to be with her that way.

Luckily, she had not refused. She hadn't admitted her desire for him in very romantic terms, he recalled with a wince. But she had at least admitted to wanting him, too. It was a start. A small step in an uphill struggle. A journey that sometimes seemed to him as

daunting as scaling Mount Everest. Little by little, day
by day, he'd make it. By some miracle, Laurel had
returned to his life—and by some even greater miracle, she was actually his wife. Now he had a year to
convince her that he loved her more than anything in
the world—and always had.

He'd tried to explain his side of the rupture in their
relationship. He'd tried to understand why she seemed
to think of herself as the wounded one. But she just
wouldn't talk it through with him. Didn't seem to
think he had the right to know. In some ways, she
wasn't the same woman he'd known. She was far less
trusting, less open about her feelings.

Had her marriage to Parson done this to her? he
wondered. Connor had heard that her ex-husband had
played around and he hated the man for it. Yet, sometimes he wondered if he was to blame for these
changes. For when Laurel spoke of their past, however much she tried to hide her feelings, he sensed
her despair, her disappointment. She seemed disillusioned. Even sad. And cynical.

But he now believed her when she claimed she'd
never read his letter, never even knew of its existence.
He wondered if his father had been involved in the
letter's disappearance. His father had known that he
and Laurel had been together on the beach that night.
When Connor had not returned home, and the party
was obviously over, Owen had come looking for him.
As the estate caretaker, it was not all that unusual for
Owen to go out late at night and check the grounds.
Especially after a party.

When Connor had returned home, Owen had been
waiting for him. Their confrontation had been bitter
and brutal. Owen had mocked his son, telling him he

was a fool to believe that a rich girl like Laurel could ever settle for a pauper. And even if she did run off with him, Owen continued, how long did Connor think it would last? How long would she go without the pampered life she was used to? And when that line of reasoning failed to sway Connor, his father had started working on his son's sense of responsibility. First, toward Charles Sutherland, whom Owen claimed would be devastated by Connor's betrayal.

"Sure, he thinks you're a fine fellow now. But do you really think her father is going to slap you on the back and hand you an imported cigar for seducing his dear daughter the night before her wedding to a fellow who could buy and sell you ten times over?" he asked with a cruel laugh.

"And what about me?" Owen continued without letup. "Did you give a thought to me—or only to your own pleasure? I'll be fired from this place, you know. After nearly twenty years of serving those rich bastards, hand and foot. And that pension he's promised me if I stayed to retirement...do you think he'll be handing over that free cash to the father of the boy who ruined his daughter's life?"

Connor argued with his father until dawn, until he was hoarse and sick at heart.

Finally, he couldn't stand to hear any more. His father had always criticized him for what he considered Connor's social climbing. As if working to be anything different than a fisherman or car mechanic was a mortal sin. Owen had always warned him that fraternizing with the Sutherlands would come to no good—that they would be kind and nice to him, but someday, when it really mattered most, they'd toss him out on his ear like a dog. And rich women use men like you for toys, to pass away their boredom, Owen reminded him. Didn't Connor think that his father knew all about that?

Try as he did to keep the acid words from affecting his judgment, somehow, drop by drop, his father's doubts and cynicism burned tiny holes in Connor's bright visions.

He decided that there was some truth to his father's fears, but only to the extent that Laurel had to be free to make up her mind, to make her own choice, without him pressuring her. He sat down and wrote her a letter, pouring out his heart, restating his love and commitment to her in no uncertain terms, but also, leaving her free to honor her promise to Todd if that was what she finally needed to do.

Then, at daybreak, he packed up his weekend bag and left his family's cottage. He dropped off the letter at Laurel's house, slipping it under the front door where he knew she would find it, or someone else in the household would doubtlessly give it to her.

He returned to New York City…and waited. Waited for her call, or letter. Any word from her at all. No word ever came. He thought about calling her but decided that her silence was perhaps eloquent enough. Two weeks later, he saw the announcement of her marriage in the *New York Times* social pages— and immediately ran into the bathroom and was sick to his stomach.

So many feelings after that, he reflected grimly. Anger, confusion, bitterness. Then denial that he'd ever felt anything real for her. He'd tried to forget her over the years and tried to minimize her meaning to him. But no other woman had ever taken her place.

She was changed from the girl he'd known as a child, and from the young woman he'd loved.

Yet the changes that had dulled her spirit made him love her even more somehow. He was determined to bring back the light of happiness and serenity to her beautiful smile. He was determined that his love would renew her. Restore her.

A year should be enough time, he assured himself. At least she still desired him and their lovemaking had been more spectacular than ever. And that was saying something. She must still feel something for him, he reasoned. He knew how he felt, holding her right now in his arms this way, knowing that she was really and truly his wife. He felt like the luckiest man in the world. He was certainly the happiest.

He would make her happy, too. Holding her this way, he felt unbeatable. Unstoppable. She might fight him at every turn, but Connor promised himself he'd win. He'd win back her trust, her respect—her deep and abiding love. For now that Laurel was finally and truly his wife, he knew he couldn't live without her.

Six

At precisely 9:00 a.m. on Monday, the board of directors of Sutherland Enterprises gathered at an emergency meeting to discuss the resignation of Phillip Sutherland.

Laurel entered with the others, trying to chat amiably and act far more relaxed than she felt. The twelve board members had been informed on Friday, by letter, of Phillip's plans. And they would soon hear Phillip's brief statement and then, hopefully, approve Laurel as the new chief executive officer and chairman of the board.

While she knew the vote was largely a formality, she couldn't help but feel jittery. If there was some doubt as to her ability to run the firm, it would place a major obstacle in her plans to repay the debt and keep Phillip out of jail. The idea of heading the corporation sometimes scared the living daylights out of her, she had to admit, but the alternative seemed even worse. Especially since she had already married Connor.

Phillip sat at the head of the long polished table and Laurel took the seat to his right. He rose to speak, and Laurel studied him as he addressed the board. Though Phillip was as well dressed as ever, his complexion looked pale, his eyes shadowed by dark circles. He had claimed his decision to step down was due to poor health, and no one looking at him at that moment seemed to doubt his explanation. The board members did not pose any questions and soon it was time to vote on Phillip's proposal that Laurel be approved as the new chairman.

The vote was anonymous and each board member jotted down a response on a slip of paper. Phillip's secretary, Miranda, collected the ballots and two board members were nominated to tally the votes. Phillip looked over at her and squeezed her hand but didn't speak. Laurel smiled reassuringly in response. She felt the eyes of everyone in the room fixed on her and tried to appear relaxed and unflustered.

Dressing for the meeting earlier that morning, Laurel had been extremely careful of her appearance. She was outfitted in a charcoal grey coat-dress ensemble, with her hair pulled back in a tight, smooth roll. The only jewelry she wore was a pair of gold earrings and her wedding rings. She looked thoroughly corporate and commanding. It was hard to believe that she'd come straight from her honeymoon suite—straight from Connor's torrid lovemaking, more precisely—to this intimidating scene.

For a moment, she wished that Connor was present. She imagined sharing a silent glance with him that would calm her jagged nerves. She had to begrudgingly acknowledge that he'd really been there for her. Though she hadn't admitted her fears to him about this meeting, Connor had sensitively boosted her courage a number of times while she dressed. He had promised her that it would go smoothly and she'd do perfectly as the new CEO. "A million times better than your brother ever did, I'd bank on it. And every one of the board members feels the same," he'd told her.

Laurel had often thought she'd have been a better choice to take over the firm. There were so many things she'd have done differently. She'd never have gotten the family into such jeopardy, for one thing. But there was a big difference between being a backseat driver and actually getting behind the wheel. If the board approved her, she'd be in the driver's seat, making the important decisions, taking the big risks.

The ballots had been counted and checked. Phillip's secretary handed him the results on a sheet of paper. He stood before announcing them, making it impossible for Laurel to get an advanced reading on her fate.

"Eleven in favor. One opposed. In keeping with the corporation's bylaws, Laurel Sutherland-Northrup is hereby elected the new chairman. Congratulations, Laurel," Phillip said. He smiled and politely extended his hand.

Laurel shook her brother's hand, and then, at his urging, they switched places at the table so that she now stood at the head. The board members softly applauded. All but one. She wasn't positive, of course, that he had voted against her, but she had already suspected. Gerald O'Kane, who was in his late seventies, still didn't believe women belonged in the workplace and made no secret of it. Well, she'd make a believer of him, Laurel silently promised as she met the old man's eyes.

The days passed incredibly quickly once Laurel began her new job. She started her workday early, sometimes arriving at the office as early as seven and leaving at nine, or even later.

Connor seemed to understand the pressure she was under, and never complained, unless to express concern for her health. Still, she wondered from time to time if he thought she kept such long hours at the office just to avoid him. Yet he never even hinted as much and was always waiting for her when she got home, interested to hear about her day, and the latest mess she'd uncovered. If she hadn't already gobbled down some vile take-out meal at her desk, Connor would serve her a simple dinner—a sandwich or an omelet—and they'd sit together and share their day over a glass of wine.

It always seemed to Laurel that she did most of the talking. Even though being a chatterbox was uncharacteristic of her, she always had a lot to tell. And most of it wasn't very good news.

Unfortunately, the missing funds were the worst, but not the only, problem that Phillip had hidden from her. During her first weeks in the job, she told Connor about various knotty situations, and his advice proved insightful, wise and, sometimes, invaluable.

Yet, he managed to talk the problems through with her in a light-handed manner, helping her see the big picture and pointing out her options. Laurel never felt condescended to, or second-guessed. And he never

failed to congratulate her on the small and large tri-
umphs she achieved on her own along the way.

At times, when they talked over such matters, Laurel felt as if the clock had turned back to a distant
time, when their easy, flowing rapport had made her
feel so in synch with Connor, closer to him perhaps
than anyone in the world. That was the way it should
feel all the time when you're married to someone,
she'd think. When you're in love with someone. But
sadly, she'd then remember that it was only during
these business chats that she had that old feeling, and
only because she and Connor did think alike when it
came to practical, business matters.

It hardly meant that he was in love with her—or
she with him.

And some nights, there was little talk. Or none. As
soon as she came home, Connor would take her in
his arms and soothe away the tense knots in her neck
and shoulders with a massaging touch that Laurel
found positively addictive. And irresistible.

One touch would lead to another, and before long,
no matter how depleted in body, mind and spirit she'd
felt walking through the door, she'd soon find herself
relaxed and eager to respond to his exciting embrace.
No matter how she'd silently insisted to herself that
she was just too exhausted to make love to Connor
that night, her inhibitions would quickly melt away.

Sometimes during even the most hectic day, Laurel
would find her mind wandering, recalling the most
passionate, most intimate moments of her nights in
Connor's arms. Deep in her own heart, she could admit how much she secretly longed for him, how eager
she was for the day to pass and darkness to fall so
that she could lose herself again in their sumptuous

sensual feasting. For, every encounter, it seemed, was unique and their compelling need for each other seemed to encompass itself in an infinite variety of expressions.

At one time before their marriage, Laurel had thought that if Connor's real motive was sexual surrender, he might grow tired of her sooner than he thought. Yet, there seemed no end to their mutual desire for each other, with each session of lovemaking taking them to even greater heights.

Once or twice, in a quiet moment, Connor tried to talk to Laurel about the past again. Each time, she successfully rebuffed his efforts. As far as she was concerned, what was past, was past. She had made her deal with him and now she would stick with it until the year's end. Wasn't it enough that she'd married him? Why did he persist in trying to get her to understand and even excuse the way he'd hurt her?

After her appointment as CEO, Laurel even went to the office on Saturdays. She knew that most other newly married men would be annoyed at such workaholic habits, but Connor was amazingly understanding. He even accompanied her on several occasions, and together, they caught up on her workload twice as fast—and much more enjoyably than it would have been all alone in empty offices, Laurel realized. One afternoon, a cleanup of some old, outdated files turned into a free-for-all paper-ball fight, and during the battle, their rough play landed them on the floor in a tumble of arms and legs. Before long, their giddy, breathless tussling turned into breathtaking caresses, and Laurel found herself making passionate love with Connor on the floor behind her desk.

As their bodies joined and moved as one, Laurel clung to him, and in some distant, foggy part of her mind she realized a simple but stunning fact: she was happy. Happier than she'd been in years. In the last seven years to be precise. But she was wise enough now to know that this moment was as fleeting and ephemeral as it was precious. Something to store away and remember once Connor was gone again.

On Sundays, Connor put his foot down. Laurel was not allowed to do any office work at all—he even frowned upon her answering the phone. Laurel usually slept late and woke to find her husband already up sipping coffee and reading the Sunday newspapers.

They'd often spend the morning walking in the park, browsing through some interesting off-the-beaten-path neighborhood or playing tennis at Connor's club—a sport they both enjoyed and had played together almost every summer day as children. Connor still had a vicious first serve, but Laurel found she was still able to handle it. She still knew how to sink one in the corner and win her point every time. Connor soon remembered how to psych her out at the net.

They'd have a late brunch, then spend the rest of the day at a museum. Or take in one of the esoteric foreign films Laurel loved so much. They would grab a light dinner out, at some out-of-the-way café or hip storefront restaurant. Connor had a penchant for spicy ethnic food that Laurel had never known about before—Indian, Thai and Cuban were his favorites. The hotter the better, he claimed. He never complained after such a spice fest and Laurel marveled at his cast-iron stomach.

His hidden talent to digest just about anything came in handy, she discovered, when she'd tried her hand at cooking a few times. Her family had always employed a cook while she was growing up and Laurel had never had a chance to test her skills in the kitchen. As an adult, she'd rarely had the time to cook—or the motivation to work on some fancy recipe just for herself. But cooking was a pastime she found very relaxing and she also liked buying the necessary kitchen gadgets or seeking out some exotic ingredient. Unfortunately, not all her efforts were successful, and sometimes she and Connor would take a bite or two, look at each other, and just laugh.

From time to time, Connor would plan a weekend for them out of the city. Laurel was not surprised to learn that he now piloted his own private plane. As a boy, he'd often said that learning to fly was one of his ambitions. For short trips, they would fly to the posh oceanfront village of Long Island's east end, Sag Harbor, or the Hamptons. If they had a long weekend, they'd fly south, to Cape Hatteras or Nag's Head in North Carolina. Connor had a knack for finding elegant old inns and seemed able to guess her preferences perfectly. Their weekends away always made Laurel feel renewed and carefree. Most of all, she felt as if Connor truly took care of her—a feeling she hadn't known in a long time.

But whether they'd spent the weekend in the city or in the country, Sundays would usually end with coffee and dessert at their favorite neighborhood coffee bar. They had a special table by the window, perfect for people watching—a great sport in their offbeat neighborhood. They'd sit there quietly, not saying much at all. Sometimes Connor would take her hand in both his own and study it with the most thoughtful expression. She always wondered what he was thinking then, but was actually afraid to ask. Besides, she didn't want to spoil the moment.

While Connor was a wonderful conversationalist, he didn't need to talk all the time. Not like some men she'd known, Laurel noticed. She had always liked that about him and appreciated the trait even more now, since she was the same way.

At the end of the weekend, she sometimes felt melancholy that her time alone with Connor was coming to an end.

And that feeling, Laurel knew, could only mean one thing. Despite her resolve to remain at a safe emotional distance, they were growing closer. And Laurel didn't like the feeling. She didn't like it at all. If I feel this blue watching a weekend come to an end, how will I feel when the year's over? she wondered. It was easier to pull away at such moments, to be cold and distant to him. As Laurel saw it, it was her only defense. The only problem with that strategy was, as time went on, it became harder and harder for Laurel to carry it out.

They had been married about three months when Connor asked her to accompany him to a formal dinner his firm was hosting.

Laurel wasn't quite sure what the occasion was— the promotion or retirement of some vice president, most likely. She disliked such corporate functions, and making a public appearance as Connor's wife put her off even more. For his sake, she decided to agree without a fuss. He had gone out of his way ever since their marriage to accommodate her, in so many ways, she thought it was only fair that she comply to his small request without complaint.

Once she thought about it, Laurel decided that it would be fun to see Connor on his own turf for once. She knew only too well that he possessed a forceful, intense personality. It would be interesting to see him in action on his own corporate playing field.

It was a formal affair, in a large, private room at a new restaurant so upscale and exclusive that Laurel had been unable to get a reservation there for the past year. She and Connor arrived after many of the guests had already gathered. As Laurel stepped through the doorway and faced a sea of unfamiliar faces, she unconsciously gripped Connor's arm a bit tighter. "Relax, you'll do fine. Everyone's dying to meet my whirlwind-romance bride."

Laurel offered Connor a brief smile, though somehow his words didn't ease her anxiety. She disliked pretense of any kind and didn't feel comfortable playing the role of a love-struck newlywed. Though she had to admit, as Connor began to introduce her to his guests, with his arm encircling her waist and a look of pride lighting his handsome face, *he* seemed more than comfortable in the role. He seemed to positively bask in it.

While anyone else in the room would have called it pure devotion, Laurel knew better. She knew his close embrace and proud introductions of his "wife" were designed to keep his business associates from suspecting anything less than a love match. Besides, she was his trophy wife. Tonight, he'd show her off as his prized possession.

Laurel had dressed for the part, even going so far as to purchase a new gown made of a liquidy, silver fabric that clung to her slim form and subtly glittered when she walked. Her shoulders and arms were covered by a sheer, illusion fabric and her hair was done in a high-style upsweep. Diamond-solitaire earrings and a diamond and sapphire tennis bracelet—Connor's Valentine's Day gift—completed her look.

Connor's look of approval, when she'd stepped into the living room after dressing, had been worth a thousand words. Of course, he'd complimented her profusely as well, which made Laurel feel the effort had been worth it.

As Laurel had guessed, the corporate side of Connor was smooth and sophisticated, totally confident yet understated. He had always shown good manners, but his social style now was so much more, she reflected. She had to admit that he was an extraordinary man in so many ways, and for a moment, she surrendered herself to the fantasy of their marriage, immersing herself in the role of Connor's wife. If only it were true, she reflected, watching him from a short distance as he stepped forward to graciously greet an older couple. How lucky she'd be...and how proud.

While Laurel had expected to see Connor mingling and networking with his business associates, she'd never expected to confront his romantic past as well. But when a tall, curvaceous brunette entered the room and literally zeroed in on Connor—as if equipped with high-tech sonar—Laurel broke out in gooseflesh. And when the stunning woman presented herself, dressed in a black satin, off-the-shoulder gown that displayed her assets to perfection, Laurel held her breath as she waited to see her husband's reaction. There was no mistaking the look of unabashed male appreciation as he smiled in greeting. He looked irritatingly at ease when the dark-haired beauty flung herself into his arms for a hello kiss.

Seems they know each other, Laurel thought. Intimately.

Laurel stood back watching—and despite herself, silently seething—as Connor and the gorgeous brunette chatted away. Catching up on old times, she'd guess. And when was he going to introduce the little wife? she wondered. Or would he skip that social nicety this time?

Finally, Connor looked away from his companion and his gaze met Laurel's. He waved, urging her to join him. As Laurel approached, she took a swift silent inventory of her rival. She couldn't imagine a woman more opposite in looks, style or attitude.

The woman swung around to greet her and then, before Laurel could even speak, clasped her in a tight hug. "And you must be Lauren—"

"Laurel," Laurel corrected. A heavy cloud of perfume engulfed her and she struggled to keep from coughing.

"Well, congratulations, Laurel—I'm so happy for you!" the woman squealed as she finally let Laurel go.

"Why, thank you… I'm sorry. I don't believe I caught…?" Laurel's voice trailed off in a question mark.

"Amanda Darling." The woman smiled, revealing perfect dimples in her gorgeous face, and dazzling white teeth. "Connor and I go *way* back. Don't we, Con?" She laughed and glanced at Connor with a sexy, knowing look that grated on Laurel's last nerve.

"We sure do," he agreed. Then he smiled at Amanda with an expression Laurel found extremely goofy. Thankfully, it quickly turned more serious. "Amanda worked for the firm for a long time. Until she left us to set up her own shop. And you're doing quite well, too, I understand. Giving us some competition," he added in a complimentary tone.

Laurel had been hoping that gorgeous Amanda didn't possess much in the way of brains or professional success. But it seemed Amanda Darling had it all—and didn't mind if the world knew it, from the looks of her very low neckline.

"What a nice thing to say, Connor. Though everyone knows you're still the *best*—and always will be in my book." Amanda gave a sexy laugh as she rested her hand on his sleeve. Finally, she spared a glance at Laurel. "I just had to meet the woman who hooked Connor. How did you ever do it? If you don't mind me asking. I think I must have tried every trick in the book," she admitted in a girl-to-girl stage whisper.

Connor laughed again and Laurel felt a major headache coming on. "Simple. It was blackmail," Laurel confessed with a totally serious expression. She took great satisfaction in knowing that her reply was the honest truth. Although Amanda could have no idea of that—or that Connor had been the blackmailer. For a moment, she thought her new husband was going to choke on his drink.

"Blackmail?" Amanda smiled at Laurel's witty comeback. "Darn, wish I'd thought of that." Her lovely face wore a pretty pout as she glanced back at Connor. He stared down into his drink, avoiding Amanda's wide-eyed gaze, and Laurel even thought she saw him blushing.

"Well, there's always next time," Laurel sympathized. Connor suddenly gave her a curious stare, as if to ask, "With Amanda's next target—or when you decide to recycle me?"

"I'll remember that," Amanda replied. Finally, she released Connor's arm. "Well good luck, Connor... But don't lose my number," she added in a joking manner.

Connor laughed easily, then moved closer to Laurel and slipped an arm around her waist. Was he trying to show Amanda that she was too late...or merely trying to protect himself? Laurel wondered with a silent laugh. Laurel felt her smile, stiff and fake on her face.

"Amanda likes to joke around, but we're really just old friends," Connor said quietly as they both watched the woman go.

"Really, Connor. You don't have to lie to me. She's the first of your former lovers I've run into, but I'm sure she won't be the last."

Connor laughed again. "You make it sound as if you expect to see hundreds of them, marching down Fifth Avenue."

"Well, I'm sure you haven't been celibate for the past seven years."

"Not quite, no," he admitted with a wry grin. Then his expression grew serious again. "But there is a world of difference between having sex and making love," he said quietly. He gave her a gentle squeeze. "Wouldn't you agree?"

"Yes, of course." Laurel looked away. She didn't know what else to say. Of course she agreed with him. But why had he bothered to point out the difference?

Did he mean that he hadn't been in love with

Amanda Darling—or whoever he'd been dating these past years—but he did love *her?* Or, did he mean to say that, years ago, he and Laurel had only shared a sexual encounter—and that was all that existed between them now as well?

Another group of guests greeted Connor, and Laurel fell back into her party persona again. The night sped by and soon they were home, preparing for bed. As Laurel sat before the mirror and brushed out her hair, she considered asking Connor what he'd meant by his cryptic comment. But then she saw his image in the mirror. He stood behind her, his hair slicked back wet from his shower, a towel tied around his waist. "You looked so beautiful tonight, Laurel," he said quietly. "I was just thinking how I must be the envy of every man at the party right now."

Laurel didn't answer. She never knew what to say when Connor came out with such statements. She merely accepted his words, reminding herself that, like many men, he knew how to warm a woman up with flattery. And even if he did think her beautiful, that still didn't amount to being in love with her, did it? Now she knew that he was quite meticulous in his thinking about such distinctions.

Connor gently took the silver-back brush from her hand and began brushing her hair, his large strong hands smoothing the tight muscles of her nape and shoulders. She watched him in the mirror, taking secret pleasure in the chance to study his bare physique—his broad chest covered with swirls of soft dark hair, his muscular shoulders. The sight and feeling of his body was familiar to her now—but as exciting as ever.

"I've always loved your hair," he confessed as he

worked. "It feels like silk. You should wear it down more often."

"Like Amanda Darling?" Laurel asked.

Connor laughed. "She really got under your skin, didn't she?"

"Don't be silly." Laurel huffed.

He put down the brush, rested his hands on her shoulders, then bent down and whispered in her ear. "I think you're the one who's being silly, Laurel. Very, *very* silly."

She felt his warm breath on her ear, then his lips, raining soft kisses on her bare shoulders. Her head dropped to one side as he smoothed away her hair and kissed her neck. His hands glided under her arms and covered her breasts, kneading her taut nipples through the silk fabric of her nightgown.

Laurel's breath caught in the back in her throat and she closed her eyes. He slipped the thin straps of her gown off her shoulders and she sat bare to her waist, his warm hands moving over her, drawing her away like the pull of a sensual sea.

When he spoke again, his husky whisper in her ear seemed to reach her from worlds away. "If I had wanted to marry Amanda, I would have," she heard him say. "But I married *you.*"

Then there was no further need for words as she surrendered herself to his thrilling touch.

Late one Friday evening Laurel remained working at her desk, as one by one the offices at Sutherland Enterprises grew empty. She had hardly even noticed that it was past five since, with the approaching spring weather, the days were growing longer and there was still an hour or more before sunset.

After Emily said goodbye and wished her a good weekend, Laurel sat gazing out the wide window near her desk that framed a magnificent view of the city from the thirtieth floor of the Sutherland Building in mid-Manhattan. Directly to the west, she could see Central Park and was amazed at how it suddenly looked green again. It was late April and she'd been married to Connor now for a little over three months. During those weeks, she had taken pleasure in seeing so many familiar traits in him, reminders of the boy she used to know. But there had also been so many new things to learn about him, things she'd never expected.

Laurel had to admit—if only to herself—that she was no longer sorry she'd married him. At first, she'd felt coerced into it and resented the way he'd manipulated her. But she knew that deep down in her heart, she was secretly storing away her memories, day by day—the hours of lovemaking, the sound of his laughter, the intimate looks and gestures that were hers alone.

Deep down in her heart, she knew that she would cherish the memories of these months with Connor. When they had first made their agreement, a year had sounded like a life sentence to her. Now she knew that a hundred lifetimes would never be enough time to be by his side.

Did that mean she had fallen in love with him all over again? Laurel sighed. The truth was, she had never stopped loving him. Not really. But in the larger picture, her love for him didn't change a thing. In most ways, it only made the situation worse. For she was sure that despite his plentiful desire, his feelings for her were only skin deep. They didn't reach his heart. If they did, why hadn't he told her that he loved her? He'd had plenty of chances to do so.

The only question in her mind now was, who would call the marriage off first? She knew that under the circumstances, she would not stay any longer than the year's time to which they'd agreed. However, she did often fear that Connor would tire of her even sooner. Men had a way of losing interest in their catch as soon as the chase was well and truly over. She didn't expect Connor to be any different.

He'd never talked about his romantic past—and except for the episode with Amanda Darling—she'd never asked him. But she was almost certain he'd had his pick of the most beautiful and exciting women in the city—and changed partners frequently. Even if familiarity didn't breed contempt in this case, it would certainly breed boredom. It was hard to imagine that his desire for her wouldn't be sated soon enough.

Laurel was so deep in her thoughts that she didn't notice when Connor entered her office. He cleared his throat noisily, and she spun around in her high-back leather chair. She hadn't planned on him meeting her at the office, but he often dropped by at the end of the day on his way home and surprised her.

"You look like you're thinking some deep thoughts tonight, Laurel. I hope you didn't find another nasty mess left by Phillip?" he asked as he stood in front of her desk.

"Uh, no. Not at all." She met his glance briefly, then looked down at the papers on her desk. "I was just thinking about the future," she murmured.

"The future, eh?" His dark eyes lit with interest.

"My schedule for next week, I mean," she explained, covering her tracks. She suddenly noticed that he wasn't wearing the suit he'd had on for work that morning. He now wore a dark blue sweater, jeans and a leather jacket. "Did you go home and change already?"

"Changed, packed and loaded the car for the weekend."

"Loaded the car...are you going someplace?" She felt a smile forming on her lips, and tried unsuccessfully to hold it back.

"*We* are going someplace...." He walked around the desk, stood beside her chair. "But don't ask me, because I won't tell you where. It's a surprise."

"You know I hate surprises," she said, although it wasn't entirely true. She actually always loved Connor's surprises.

"Don't worry. You'll like this one," he promised. With a swift, firm motion, he spun around her chair until she was facing him. She looked up. He seemed incredibly tall.

Still, she knew he was vulnerable to her... incredibly vulnerable at times.

"I have my ways of making you talk, you know," she said with a small, sexy smile.

"Oh, you think so, do you?" he replied with a challenging grin. "Such as?"

"Such as this," she said. Hooking her finger in his belt, she pulled him closer. He laughed in surprise, a deep, warm sound. Encouraged by his reaction, she lifted the edge of his sweater and ran the tip of her tongue along the waistband of his jeans, where the denim met his bare skin. The muscles in his abdomen instantly tightened and she heard his deep growl of pleasure.

"And this," she murmured against his firm, flat belly as she continued her assault.

His grip on her shoulders tightened. "Laurel...please," he sighed. "Let's just save that thought for later...when we get there... Laurel?..."

Still, he seemed unable, or unwilling, to push her away and she continued her subtle, sexy torture. She didn't understand why she always felt so wanton and uninhibited with Connor. She'd never been this way before. It was as if another woman had taken over her body.

"And where, may I ask, is *there?*" she whispered between seductive licks and wet kisses. Despite his resolve, his hips moved forward, seeking the warmth of her mouth. She unsnapped the top of his jeans and pulled down the elastic edge of his underwear. She loved the taste of his warm skin, his special scent. The grip on her shoulders became leaden as he held her for support.

"Uh-uh..." His voice faltered. "Can't...tell," he mumbled in a tight voice.

"Tell me," she coaxed. "Please?..." The sight of his burgeoning male hardness outlined beneath the denim excited her as she caressed him with her hand, her tongue dipping lower and lower, her mouth finally found him and took him inside.

"Laurel...honey," he groaned. "I want it to be a-ah-h-h-h...a surpri—Oh, don't stop. Yes...yes...oh, yes. Yes."

He groaned with satisfaction and gritted his teeth, his fingertips digging into her shoulders. Then suddenly he let go and dropped in a heap next to her chair. With a deep sigh, he rested his head on her lap.

She gave him a moment to recuperate. "You're

tough. Aren't you going to tell me now?'' she persisted.

"I was afraid if I told you, you'd stop,'' he admitted, gasping for air. ''I'm taking you up to the Cape…. Damn it, woman, what did you do to me?'' He laughed huskily as he fumbled to fix his clothing.

"I told you I had my ways.'' She rested her hand on his thick hair, stroking his dark mane with her fingertips as she considered his announcement.

She wasn't sure if she wanted to go up to New England. Did Connor think he'd get her to visit her estate on the Cape? The house was closed and had been rarely used in the past years. When she was married to Todd, he never liked going up there and always wanted to spend their free time exploring new places.

Once Phillip and Liza had children, they'd gone there much more than Laurel, even after she was single again. She'd rightfully been a half owner of the estate after her father's death but often felt as if she was a guest, intruding on Phillip's private family time when they all stayed there together.

Now she owned it all and Connor had insisted that the title be transferred to her name alone, not jointly owned with him. Still, it seemed to be so important to him that Phillip sign over his share. Yet, after their marriage, he'd never mentioned it. Was he thinking of it though? Thinking of the past? He had some sort of romantic pilgrimage in mind, she was sure, and she didn't know if she felt up to it. They could never go back and rewrite the past, erase the pain and heartache of so many years. It would only make things worse, Laurel thought.

He stood up. ''Everything's ready,'' he said,

though she knew from the look on his face he had sensed her hesitation. "I've got the car double-parked. We'd better go."

She would have to face the place sooner or later, she reasoned. But not now, she decided. After she'd lost him again. After their marriage was all over and done. She couldn't go there again now, knowing she was only going to lose him again.

"I'll go someplace with you," she said as she stood up. "But not to the Cape."

"Why not?" Connor asked. "You know we're not staying at the house. Though I thought we could go by and check on it."

"That's exactly what I suspected," Laurel said sharply. "And exactly what I don't want to do. I mean it, Connor. I won't go up there with you. Don't try to talk me into it, either."

"You own the place now, Laurel. Lock, stock, and barrel. Don't you think you ought to take a look at it? For pity's sake, the real estate is worth a fortune and the house could be falling to pieces for all you know."

"I pay someone well to keep a very watchful eye on the house and property. You know that, Connor," she retorted. "When and if I go up there is my business. It has nothing to do with you."

"It has everything to do with me, Laurel. It has everything to do with us. Don't you see?"

"I don't know what you're talking about," she argued back, though in truth, she knew very well what he meant.

"We have to face the past, Laurel. We have to go back before we can go forward. Don't you see that I only thought it might be easier for us there?'' he confessed. ''There are good things to remember, too.''

She understood what he was saying but would not give up her ground. To go back, to open old wounds—perhaps on that very beach where they had first made love—it all seemed too frightening to her. She didn't want to hear his explanations. She knew she wouldn't believe them.

She stood facing him, her hands on her hips. She could tell by the look on his face, he had expected some resistance, but thought he'd be able to persuade her.

''I don't see any point to it,'' she challenged him. ''You talk as if we have a future together. But our agreement was only for a year—and it's nearly half over.''

She could see his expression darken and grow cold. Her bitter words had hurt him, but she wouldn't pretend that they really had a future together. Didn't he see how much that pretense hurt her?

''Is it?'' he asked coolly. ''I haven't been watching the calendar that closely. Though you seem to be counting the days.''

Yes, she had been counting the days. But not at all the way he thought. Still, she couldn't admit that to him now. She wouldn't dare show him her true feelings about their marriage.

''I won't go,'' she said calmly. ''You can go by yourself if you wish. I won't stop you.''

They'd locked horns before, plenty of times. But this was their first full-blown argument. If she'd had to bet on the outcome in advance, she would have picked Connor as the winner. But, here they stood, in a face-off, and amazingly, she could see his expression change to one of resignation.

He looked down at the floor briefly and shoved his hands into his jacket pockets. "All right, Laurel. We'll revise the flight plan." He paused and took a deep breath. "How about Saratoga? We've never been there together."

She loved Saratoga and hadn't been there in a long time. The main street was charming, with loads of antique stores that had bargain prices compared to prices in the city. The restaurants were great, too. Not to mention a dip in the springs. Sure to wash away any lingering hard feelings, she hoped.

"Saratoga sounds good to me. Did you pack my bathing suit?"

"No, I didn't think of it…but I'd be happy to take you shopping for one—"

The angry look on his face had melted away, replaced by one far more relaxed and even playful.

"Thanks, but I think I can manage on my own," she replied with a small smile. She was sure that Connor's idea of attractive swimwear for her would be very close to wearing nothing at all.

"Shucks…" He shook his head in dismay. "Well, maybe I'll surprise you with one then." He stepped toward her and rested his hands on her shoulders.

She looked up at him. "I think we've had enough surprises for one weekend, don't you?" she asked quietly, meaning not only his idea of sorting out the past, but their argument as well.

He met her gaze and solemnly nodded, as if he'd read her mind.

Then he suddenly flashed a sexy grin. She could tell he was thinking now of their recent red-hot encounter. ''They weren't *all* bad, Laurel. Come to think of it, I'd hate to have you mad at me all weekend.''

Laurel had to smile then, feeling thankful that their tense moment had passed. And the sensual tone of his voice was almost as thrilling as the deep, warm kiss that followed.

Seven

Laurel waited for Connor to ask her again to travel up to the estate, or even to maneuver her into talking about the past. But weeks went by and he never mentioned the subject. She often wondered about the letter he'd claimed he'd written to her. Then, she would dismiss the entire notion, thinking herself foolish to even entertain such a silly, transparent excuse.

During the last week in July, Connor told Laurel he'd purchased tickets for a play she wanted to see. She was surprised when he said he'd gotten seats for a weeknight. She usually worked well past curtain time on Broadway and he very well knew it.

"Oh, come on. You can leave the office at a decent hour for once in your life, Laurel," he laughed in response to her hesitant reply. "I wanted good seats and the weekends were sold out," he explained. "Oh, and I thought we'd go to Café Des Artistes for dinner after," he added, knowing full well she'd approve. The beautiful and exclusive restaurant located near Central Park was one of her favorites, and certainly, the most romantic place she'd ever dined, though she'd never been there with Connor.

"You've planned quite a night out," she remarked. "What's the occasion?"

"Isn't a man allowed to take his wife out for a night on the town once in a while?" he replied. "Besides, you've been working way too much lately. You really have to slow down. A night out will be good for you."

While Laurel could hardly argue with his answer, she still suspected he had something up his sleeve. The play, a compelling family drama, was excellent—as good, if not better than, the rave reviews had promised. Laurel enjoyed every minute, and as the curtain dropped on the last scene, she squeezed Connor's hand in her own and glanced at him with a smile. "That was really something," she said. "Thank you."

He smiled, then leaned down to brush her cheek with a quick kiss. "You're quite welcome. I enjoyed watching *you* during the show almost as much as I enjoyed watching the actors," he said.

Laurel just smiled and began to edge her way out of the crowded theater. She felt Connor's reassuring touch on her back. She was used to his teasing by now and knew it was better not to encourage him by answering.

The restaurant was as beautiful as she remembered, and the food even better. The meal passed pleasantly, though uneventfully. Laurel left the table briefly and when she returned found a small velvet bag at her place—in addition to the coffee and dessert she had ordered.

"What's this?"

"Open it," Connor replied, suppressing a grin. Laurel simply stared at the bag for a moment. "Go on. It won't bite you."

She hesitantly picked it up and pulled opened the gold drawstring closure. She felt inside and found a pair of stunning sapphire and diamond earrings. The setting had an antique look and Laurel gasped with surprise.

"Connor—these are beautiful," she said sincerely. She picked one earring up and held it to the light. The blue and icy white stones glimmered like stars plucked from the night sky.

"I thought they'd match your engagement ring. And sapphires suit you, I think," he said thoughtfully.

"What a beautiful gift," she said, gazing at the jewels in the palm of her hand. "But why did you get me such an expensive present? It isn't my birthday—"

"I know very well when your birthday is, Laurel," he cut in. "I've already picked out the matching necklace." He gazed at her, his head to one side. "Still can't guess what today is?"

"It's not *your* birthday, I know that," she murmured, trying to figure out his puzzle. "Hmm…I really can't guess. You'll just have to tell me."

"It's our anniversary," he explained. "Six months, I mean."

"Oh—" She cleared her throat and set the earrings on the velvet bag.

She didn't know why his announcement had suddenly dampened her mood, but it definitely had. She realized full well that the halfway point was passing but didn't think he had noticed. It was not a happy day for her. Not something she wanted to celebrate, for it meant that half of her time with Connor had already passed. Obviously, he felt differently.

And the extravagant gift? A means of soothing his conscience, she suspected, for she'd felt since day one that he was uncomfortable with the way he'd manipulated her into their marriage. He'd gotten his cake and was eating it, too, yet often seemed to feel some guilty pangs about it.

"Well, we made it," was all she could manage to say. "I…uh…I didn't think to get you anything," she added.

"That's okay. I didn't expect you to," he answered. His mood had grown much more subdued as well and he seemed to be studying her carefully.

"Why don't you try them on?" he coaxed her. When she hesitated, he persisted. "Don't you like them?"

"Of course I do. They're perfect…." Her voice trailed off as she touched the jewels. "The whole evening was perfect—the theater and dinner. But you didn't have to go to so much trouble for me, Connor," she insisted.

"I know I didn't have to. I wanted to, Laurel," he replied with a wondering gaze. As if he sensed her displeasure, and withdrawal from him, but didn't quite understand. "I like to do things for you. I like to make you happy," he said simply.

Laurel stared down at the earrings and then, quite purposely, returned them to the velvet bag. "Well, it's funny because the gift is beautiful—very beautiful, honestly. And while I'm sure it would have pleased a lot of other women you've known, it didn't make me happy," she confessed. She pushed her hair back with her hand and looked up at him. "It made me feel…cheap, actually. Bought and paid for." She pushed the bag across the table toward him and left it there. "I knew what I agreed to when I married you. You don't have to buy me off—or go to such extremes to soothe your conscience."

His expression darkened like a stormy sky, his eyes narrowing to two black slits. "Is that what you think I was trying to do? Soothe my guilty conscience?"

Laurel felt her resolve falter. He looked genuinely hurt by her words. Still, she held her ground. "Only you know the answer to that question, Connor."

"Yes, only I know the answer. That's true," he replied evenly. He took the velvet pouch in his hand and rested it in his palm, as if to test the weight. "And only you know the answer to this one, Laurel—when will you stop doubting me? When will you understand that I just want to take care of you?"

Laurel had no answer. She would always doubt him, she believed. Just as she would always love him. And although he claimed to care for her, she was very aware that he'd never once said he loved her—not even in their most heated moments of passion.

"I can take care of myself," she answered finally. "Would you like me to get the check?" she offered politely.

"No, dear," he replied coldly. "This party's on me."

As their cab sped downtown through the light late-night traffic, Laurel sat in the farthest corner of the cab, putting as much distance as she could between herself and Connor. But she was tired and soon rested her head back against the seat and closed her eyes. When the cab came to a jolting stop and she opened her eyes, she realized that they had arrived home and she was somehow nestled up against her husband, with his hand lazily stroking her hair. She had worn it down for him, in the loose casual style he liked so much.

She was embarrassed at first to find herself in his embrace, after her angry words in the restaurant. But as they rode up to their apartment in tense silence, she decided to forgive herself for the lapse. She'd be without the comfort of his arms enough, after their marriage ended, in the long, lonely years ahead.

The years ahead without Connor might not be so lonely, Laurel realized one evening with a jolt. And she would have more to remember him by than a collection of expensive jewelry.

As Laurel stared down at the blue dot on the home pregnancy kit, she could not believe her eyes. The test, which promised to be nearly foolproof, registered proof positive that she was pregnant. And so had the last three.

She hadn't been alarmed when she noticed her period was late. She'd never been all that regular, and stressful situations sometimes threw her inner clock off entirely.

No wonder she'd been so exhausted these last few weeks. No wonder the smell of certain foods made her queasy. She'd considered seeing a doctor, thinking she needed vitamins or something. Whenever the thought had crossed her mind that she might be pregnant, she had instantly dismissed it. She'd been so careful about birth control, the odds were next to impossible.

But nothing is foolproof, she realized, staring at the telling test results. And she and Connor did make love often....

Laurel sat stunned, staring out the window of her bedroom. Luckily, Connor was away on a business trip in Arizona, and she'd brought home the tests that night, knowing she'd have complete privacy. But while one part of her was relieved to be alone, the other side clamored to share the good news with someone. With Connor, of course.

The idea of having a baby—his baby—was overwhelming.

She had always wanted children. Her one regret after her marriage to Todd had been that she'd never gotten pregnant. Of course, the circumstances in their marriage weren't right for starting a family. But things were hardly any better between herself and Connor, Laurel thought, sighing aloud. She counted the months on her fingers, realizing that she'd only be four months pregnant by January, when the year's limit to their marriage arrived.

Would Connor be angry when he learned about the baby? Would he demand that they remain married for the sake of the child? She hoped not. It would be even harder to remain with him, knowing he didn't love her but played the role of a dutiful husband for the sake of their child.

If they got divorced, he seemed the type to demand shared custody of the baby—or at least ample visiting rights. Could she go on for years, connected to him through their child, yet not really connected? It was all so troubling, so complicated. Laurel couldn't imagine how she'd ever find a solution....

She sighed and rested her hand on her flat abdomen, thinking of a baby growing inside. Would she have dark hair like Connor—or be fair, like her? Laurel had to laugh at herself for already assuming the baby would be a girl. It might be a boy—a strong, spirited little boy, just like his father.

The baby was everything. Once she thought of the baby, her worries about the future vanished. She'd manage somehow. But how should she tell Connor? And when? Laurel wondered if she should even tell him at all. Perhaps she could manage to hide the pregnancy from him, and after they separated, she could simply disappear for a while, have the baby in secret and later deny that Connor was the child's father.

Did she dare deceive him that way? Could she even do such a thing to him, an act she knew would surely devastate him if he ever discovered her betrayal? No—Laurel was not now, and never had been, the vengeful type. Despite his heartless treatment of her in the past. Even despite the way he'd blackmailed her into this marriage, Laurel knew she could never retaliate in such a way. For one simple reason—she loved him.

Her love for Connor was the deepest, truest feeling she'd ever known—the rock-bottom foundation of her soul, her very existence. All her life, she'd waited to know a love like this one, limitless and unconditional, that drew her so completely out of herself.

Yet, in real life—her life—it wasn't at all the way she'd seen it in fairy tales and romantic stories. While Connor's smile took her to the heights and his slightest touch set her soul on fire, she knew very well there would be no happily-ever-after for them. There would be an ending all right, but not a happy one....

Exhausted by her worries, Laurel crawled into bed and shut the light. The big bed felt cold and empty without Connor. Even though he'd called earlier to say hello, their conversation had been brief and somewhat stilted, since she'd been so distracted by trying out her pregnancy test. At least he would be away for a few more days, giving her a chance to compose herself and get her act together.

As Laurel drifted off to sleep, she resolved that she must tell him the truth—come what may. But how—and when—remained the big question.

Connor returned from his trip to Arizona exhausted and edgy. An error in some computer software had made a mess of a huge analysis project, and the client was furious. Laurel tried to draw Connor out, hoping to provide the same kind of support he always showed her. But he spoke very little about the situation and basically brushed off her attempts to help him.

The tension between them that had begun the night Laurel refused to accept the sapphire earrings had never totally been smoothed away. And while they were always unfailingly polite to each other—and still made love long and often—they no longer shared an easy, affectionate rapport.

Laurel decided to wait until the weekend to tell him about the baby. But when the weekend arrived, she could never find quite the right time, and soon, the week passed as well, and she still hadn't told him. And then the next week passed as well, and all the while, the atmosphere between them grew colder and more distant every day.

The tension of keeping her secret, coupled with her long hours at the office and the pregnancy itself were taking their toll. Laurel dragged herself through the day, feeling exhausted, and the smell of food usually made her queasy—if not downright sick. At night, she dropped down next to Connor on their bed and just about passed out with fatigue. Connor was concerned and urged her to visit a doctor, even threatening to take her to one himself. Of course, Laurel had visited a doctor several times in the last month—though not the type he assumed she'd see.

When Connor inquired about the doctor's prognosis, she gave him a vague, half-true answer, saying, "The doctor thinks I should just slow down a bit. She says there's nothing really wrong with me…I'm just a bit overstressed."

"Overstressed?" Connor echoed. "Are you sure that's all it is? Did she give you a blood test? That sort of thing?" he persisted.

Laurel nodded innocently. "Of course. The examination was quite thorough."

Still, he looked worried. "Well, I think you spend too much time at the office. It would do you good to slow down a bit."

"Oh, I think I'll be slowing down quite a bit in the coming months," she promised him.

With the weather getting cooler once more, Laurel managed to hide the changes in her body with heavier, loose-fitting clothing. It was harder to hide her body from Connor, especially in intimate moments. But if he noticed any changes in her figure, he never commented on them. Their lovemaking had grown less frequent as well, she noticed, with a very different quality to Connor's touch. A mixture of reluctance and hunger—as if he was making love to her in spite of himself.

What did it mean? she wondered. Was he growing bored with her already? While his departure from her life would make things simple in some ways, it hurt to think that her worst suspicions about his feelings for her were true.

One afternoon, while sitting in a meeting with her department heads, Laurel felt particularly foggy-headed and distracted. Her worries about the baby and Connor seemed overwhelming and she felt so tired, all she wanted to do was sleep. She forced herself to concentrate on the discussion at hand, a review of last quarter's sales figures. But her mind wandered again. Someone asked Laurel a question and their voice seemed to come from far away. She turned her head suddenly, to look at the person who was speaking to her and the room spun...then everything went black.

When she opened her eyes again, she was lying on a couch in the meeting room. The room was now completely empty, except for her secretary. As Laurel slowly opened her eyes and struggled to sit up, the older woman peered down at her with a deeply concerned expression, then gently pressed on her shoulder so that Laurel couldn't get very far.

"Hold on a second there, boss. You aren't going anywhere," Emily ordered her.

"I can at least sit up, Em," Laurel insisted. She touched her hand to her forehead. "For goodness' sakes, I guess I fainted. That never happened to me before."

"It gets pretty stuffy in here sometimes. And

you've been looking sort of peaked lately, if you don't mind me saying so. Anything you'd like to tell me?'' Emily asked pointedly.

Laurel met her gaze, then looked away. ''Maybe I'm coming down with the flu,'' she offered.

Emily stared at her and nodded, clearly seeing through her thin lie, but having the grace not to say so. ''Well, maybe you ought to see a doctor. Shall I call the doctor for you?''

''Uh, no…I can call later. I think I'll just go home early and rest.''

''My word, miracles do happen,'' Emily exclaimed dryly, for they both knew very well that Laurel had never left the office early in her life—except perhaps for another business appointment. ''Can I help you downstairs?'' she offered gently.

Laurel was about to refuse, then nodded. She had to think about what was best for the baby now. ''Thanks, I'd appreciate that.''

''No problem,'' Emily replied. ''And don't worry about anything going on around here. Take tomorrow off and rest if you still feel tired. The place won't fall to pieces without you.''

Laurel was thankful for her concern and friendship. She felt the impulse to tell Emily about the baby— then stopped herself. Emily was a brick, but she was never able to keep a secret. By five o'clock the entire firm would know.

Emily helped Laurel up from the couch and hovered around her like a mother hen until Laurel had gathered her belongings and was safely on her way home.

Laurel had rarely been at home at this hour of the day and the apartment seemed strangely quiet and empty. She dropped her coat and briefcase on a chair in the foyer and went straight to the bedroom where she flopped fully clothed on the bed. She could smell Connor's cologne on the pillow beside her, and she sleepily curled on her side and pulled the pillow closer, hugging it to her chest.

When Laurel finally woke up, she had no idea how long she'd been asleep. The room was completely dark and it took her a few moments to remember what had happened. As sleep slowly cleared from her head, she became aware of Connor's shadowy outline, seated at the edge of the bed.

"Are you awake, Laurel?" he asked quietly. "Shall I help you get up?"

"I'm all right," she murmured. She pushed a heavy curtain of hair to one side, away from her face. "What time is it?"

"About eight o'clock," Connor replied. "I called your office and Emily told me you'd gone home sick. I came right away to check on you, but I thought I should let you sleep."

"Thanks," Laurel murmured. She wanted to touch him, to hold him. To feel him holding her. It seemed the natural thing to do. Yet, she held herself back. He hadn't touched her, she noticed, though he was sitting quite close.

"I think I'll take a shower," she said. She sat up suddenly and felt the room spin a bit. Connor reacted instantly and slipped his arm around her shoulder. "Laurel? What is it? Should I call a doctor?"

"No...no, I'm okay," she insisted. Her head cleared and she sat upright. "Honestly," she assured him when he didn't look that convinced. "I think I've just got a touch of the flu. It's going around the office. The whole place is out sick.''

She stood up and headed for the bathroom, feeling his concerned gaze fixed on her. "I'll wait right here while you're in the bathroom," he said. "Leave the door open in case you need help."

The hours of deep sleep had restored her and the shower felt wonderfully refreshing. Laurel toweled off, slipped on a long, velour lounging robe, a deep midnight blue that complemented her golden hair and blue eyes. She removed the stray pins from her hair and brushed it out so that it fell in loose waves around her shoulders. When she gazed at her reflection, she thought she looked considerably better. The dark circles under eyes had all but disappeared and her cheeks looked rosy from the shower.

She felt ready to face the world again—and to face Connor. She took a deep breath as she left the bedroom, preparing herself to deliver the news about the baby.

But her resolve began to wane once she entered the kitchen where Connor had fixed a light meal of soup and sandwiches. The table was already set and Laurel took her place as Connor served the food.

She sensed a certain undefinable tension in the air the moment her gaze met his—an unspoken tension that seemed to grow stronger as each minute in his company passed.

"Feeling any better?" he asked.

"Much better, thanks. Maybe I just needed to catch up on my sleep," Laurel replied. "I've lost that green-around-the-gills look, don't you think?" she asked him.

He glanced over at her for a moment, then away.

"I think you look absolutely beautiful. As always,'' he stated in a quiet, curiously dispassionate tone that Laurel found disconcerting.

Finally, he sat down across from her and began to eat his meal. He asked her a few more questions about her fainting episode, but she could tell that something more was on his mind.

Laurel wondered what it could be. He hadn't mentioned any business problems lately—though she had to admit, they weren't communicating all that well anymore. He might have been facing some business difficulty and hadn't bothered to confide in her, she thought with a wince.

Or perhaps it was even worse. Maybe he'd somehow found out about her pregnancy and wanted to confront her. That possibility made Laurel grow even more tense. Her reasons for keeping the pregnancy secret from him sounded so feeble when she ran through them in her mind. He'd be angry to find out about her condition and within his rights, she thought.

Well, her father had always told her that the best offense is a strong defense. Maybe she could beat him to the punch by telling him right away about the baby.

Before she could broach the topic, Connor stared across at her and pushed his plate away. "I need to speak to you about something, Laurel," he began. "Something serious."

"It sounds very serious," she replied, trying to keep her voice light. "Did I forget to put the cap on the toothpaste again?" she teased, remembering one of his pet peeves.

"No—nothing like that. I only wish it were that simple." He caught her gaze for one intense moment, and Laurel felt he could see down to the depth of her very soul. Then he looked away and took a deep breath. "It's difficult for me to say this. But I have to be honest. I want to release you from our agreement... I've begun to think this marriage was a mistake."

Laurel felt the blood rush to her feet and the room reel, but struggled not to faint again. She felt shocked, yet another part of her had seen this coming. She imagined for a moment that she'd misunderstood him, but the deadly serious expression on his face assured her that she had not.

"Laurel? Are you okay?" He reached across the table toward her, but she pulled away. "Maybe you're not well enough to talk about this now—"

"No, don't put it off," she insisted, gathering her strength. "Now that the cat's out of the bag, I want to get it over with. I'm not surprised, really," she confessed. "You've seemed very...distant lately. I guess you've been thinking about this for a while."

"For the past few weeks," he confessed. "I can't just sit by and watch you make yourself sick over this...arrangement."

Laurel tried to interrupt him but he wouldn't let her.

"Just hear me out, please," he insisted. "I guess I didn't realize just *how* unhappy you were until that night we went to the theater, and at the restaurant, you told me what you really felt." And just about threw a pair of sapphire earrings in his face, Laurel thought regretfully. "Up until then, I'd thought *sometimes* you were happy with me."

Deep lines of distress marred his strong, handsome features and Laurel wanted to reach out to him, to press her hand to his cheek. But of course, she couldn't. Her mind spun in confusion and she didn't know what to say—did he really care for her, or was he only saying this because his pride was hurt, his ego bruised that she hadn't melted at his feet? As most of his women must do, whether he tells them that he loves them, or not, she thought.

Or, maybe he was simply tired of what he considered her indifference to him. Did he want her to fall in love with him—and withhold his love from her? Was that the ultimate goal, which he now thought unattainable—or simply not worth the effort?

"I was happy with you sometimes," she confessed finally. She stared down at her hands and twisted her wedding ring. If only he would say that he loved me, she thought, then everything would be okay. I'd forgive him anything for that. She continued to stare at her rings, waiting, willing him to say the words.

"In bed, you mean?" he prodded her.

She looked up at him. "Wasn't that obvious?"

"Yes, it was obvious," he answered with a thin, ironic smile, "but ultimately, not enough, I'm afraid."

"But Connor, listen, please. It was wrong of me to turn down your gift the way I did. It was…very rude and even cruel," she admitted, trying to explain her side to him.

"But it was at least honest. You don't think I've hated the pretense between us?" he asked. "I've hated every minute of it. And I know you did, too. I also know that once you make a promise, you stick to it, Laurel. Come hell or high water. But you don't have to stay with me out of some false sense of duty. Or self-sacrifice. That's really the last thing I ever wanted," he said decisively. "I've cleaned the slate at the firm for you, as promised, and there's no need to repay me. We've had, what…almost eight months together? I'll consider the note…satisfied.''

''Was that all it was to you—a debt to be repaid?''

''Wasn't that all it meant to you?'' he countered coldly.

She could barely believe his chilly, distant tone. Talking about duty, self-sacrifice, and debts accounted for. Didn't love enter into his calculations? It did for her, tipping the scales in all the wrong directions, she could see now.

Staring into his dark cold gaze, Laurel felt suddenly and utterly sick. He didn't love her. And never would.

She couldn't bear to tell him now about the baby. Her heart was breaking all over again, though it was hard to believe that it could hurt as badly—or even worse—than it had eight years ago.

She took a long deep breath, willing herself to remain strong.

''Yes, of course,'' she said finally in a tone as brittle as ice cracking. ''It was just a deal I struck with you. You were good to help Phillip and me. For old time's sake, I suppose. But like you said, we can consider all debts paid now.'' She stood up, then pushed her chair under the table.

She could feel his gaze fixed on her, his face a stone-cold mask. He swallowed hard as she watched her leave the room, and for a moment she thought he might call her back.

But he didn't and she didn't dare turn around to take one last look at him because she didn't want him to see her cry.

Although she had cried herself to sleep, she was finally able to stop because she realized that it might be harmful to the baby. Somehow, by half past six the next morning, she was on the road, driving north and already in Connecticut. The newly risen sun was burning away the early-morning fog, and the rush-hour traffic on the parkway was just starting to thicken.

Dressed in jeans, boots and a loose sweater top, Laurel cruised at a reasonable speed, sipping some weak tea and wishing it was strong black coffee. But the doctor had warned her against the dangers of caffeine, especially early in the pregnancy. Now she meant to focus totally on the baby. It was the only distraction that could keep the pain of thinking about Connor at bay.

She had tossed and turned all night, hardly sleeping at all. Each time she opened her eyes, the other, empty side of the bed seemed to mock her, adding insult to injury.

Just a few minutes after she'd retired to the bedroom last night, she'd heard the front door slam, announcing Connor's exit. When she'd finally dragged herself out of bed at about 5:00 a.m., a quick tour of the apartment revealed that he had not come.

Laurel was stunned for a moment, then, as if on automatic pilot, she'd moved into action. She packed a duffel bag with some essentials and remembered to include her notebook computer and cell phone. She suddenly knew where she was going. The only place she could go now, it seemed. The only place that felt like home. Up to Cape Cod, to the old estate house.

Now she almost had to laugh at herself as she faced the rest of the journey. Maybe Connor was right after all when he'd told her that they had to go back before they could go forward. She had dreaded the thought then. Suddenly, it seemed to be the only choice. And she would return alone, without him, Laurel realized. The same way she would somehow manage to live the rest of her life.

Laurel didn't reach the house until late afternoon. It had rained steadily for the past several hours, causing an annoyingly tedious drive. But her spirits lifted as the house came into view and, as promised, Jake Pratt was there to meet her.

Jake, a local carpenter and all around fix-it expert, had been watching over the house for years now, ever since Owen Northrup had retired to Florida. Laurel liked Jake—he was much cheerier than the perennially dour Owen. When Laurel had called him from the road earlier that morning, Jake hadn't seemed put out at all to open the place for her on such short notice. He greeted her warmly and helped her carry in her belongings from the car.

The house had the damp, cold smell of a place that has been closed up for too long, Laurel noticed. Despite the rain, all the windows were open, letting in fresh air. Most of the cobwebs were cleared and the covers removed from the furnishings in the main rooms downstairs. A fire had been laid in the living-room hearth for later, and the kitchen was in order as well, with a few essentials in the cupboards and refrigerator.

"It's a beautiful old place," Jake commented, gazing around before he made his departure. "I must admit, I hate to see it going empty for so long. Will you be coming up this way more often from now on?" he asked.

"Uh, well...I'll be here for a while," Laurel answered vaguely. "I've been thinking of taking some time off my job and staying here, maybe through the holidays."

"Rattling around this big place all on your own? It'll be lonely for you. But I suppose your husband will be here on weekends?"

"Oh, I won't be lonely," Laurel replied, ignoring his question about Connor. "I practically grew up here. I really love it."

"Yes, I'm sure you do," Jake said amiably. "Well, if you need anything, just call. The phone service should be back on by tomorrow morning…. But I hope you don't have any emergencies?" he asked, suddenly concerned.

"I have a cell phone with me," Laurel replied.

His concern seemed satisfied by that answer and Jake finally said goodbye.

Once the heavy front door had closed behind him, Laurel felt terribly alone. But she wasn't alone, she realized with a small smile as she patted her slightly rounded abdomen. The thought of the baby lifted her spirits once more. She focused on the tasks of settling in and found herself growing more and more at ease in the old house that was so full of memories.

Instead of sleeping in her bedroom, Laurel chose a guest room on the second floor at the rear of the house, with a window that afforded an ocean view. She was dying for a walk on the beach, but it was still raining too hard. She'd heard the local weather report on the radio in the car and knew it would continue like this through tomorrow.

Down in the kitchen, she fixed herself a cup of tea and decided first to check in with her office. Emily was the only one who knew her actual whereabouts and was sworn to secrecy. While Emily knew Laurel planned to be out of the office for a few days, even she had no idea how long Laurel really planned on staying away.

While driving up to New England, Laurel had a long time to think about the events of the past year—and the consequences she would soon face. She realized that she needed time—a great deal of it—to get past these trying times. At some point, working might be a great balm to her soul, a way to get a foothold on solid ground after her divorce from Connor. It had been that way for her after her father's death.

But right now she knew she had to take a leave from the firm, or she'd be risking both her health and sanity—and the health of the baby.

It would be all sorted out in time, though, she counseled herself. She moved around the house, busily closing windows against the chilly night air that was quickly moving in. Then she lit the fire and sat beside the hearth in a favorite old armchair. She'd brought a few books with her, but nothing caught her interest.

She tossed a thick sweater across her lap, like an afghan, and closed her eyes. The painful scene with Connor from the night before immediately rushed up to fill her consciousness. What was he doing now? she wondered. Had he even returned to the apartment yet, and found her brief note? She hadn't written much to him, just that she was moving out and would return for the rest of her belongings some time later. Their separation and divorce would be quite simple actually, since—at her insistence—they had signed a prenuptial agreement. Even so, Connor had demanded terms that were far too generous in her favor, she'd always thought. Now, with the baby coming, maybe that was just as well.

The baby. He would love the baby, she was sure of that, even if he didn't love her. Connor had once told her how much he'd always wanted children. At the time, the conversation had made her uneasy. She knew that they wouldn't remain married beyond the year's end and believed that they'd never have children together. It had hurt so much for her to imagine Connor having a baby with some other woman someday. She practically couldn't stand the thought of it. So she had quickly changed the conversation to some other topic and had never told him how much she wanted children, too.

Once back in the house, Laurel had expected that she would be dwelling far too much on memories of the night she'd made love to Connor on the beach. But, oddly, that was not the case. Instead, she found herself thinking a lot about her mother. As she sat before the stone hearth, the firelight was the only light in the dark room and cast a photograph of her mother on the mantel in a golden shadow.

Her mother had been a woman who really knew how to love, Laurel reflected. She knew how to love her children and her husband. Even when it was hard to do so, she'd loved blindly and bravely. But how had she done it…and made it look so easy all the time? Laurel wondered. Perhaps it was the idea of becoming a mother herself that made Laurel reflect on these questions, she realized.

Or perhaps it was her breakup with Connor. Her mother's face in the portrait seemed to gently coax the truth from her—and comfort her. How Laurel wished she was here once more, to tell her what to do.

But she did know what to do, some inner voice reminded her. Right at that moment, thinking of her mother's loving ways, Laurel could see that she hadn't been honest with Connor. She hadn't been open and generous-hearted. She hadn't loved bravely. She'd only let Connor see the fear in her heart… instead of the bounty of love she truly felt.

You longed to hear him tell you that he loved you, she thought. You waited and never said a word. But how could you expect him to give you something that you weren't willing to give either? You have to tell him that you love him. That was your mistake in the past. It's the wrong you must make right. Nothing in your life—and in your heart—will ever feel right until you do.

Yes, she had to tell him the truth about her feelings, and she felt a great relief finally admitting that to herself. It didn't matter if he loved her or not. Love was such a precious gift—especially the kind she felt for him. The kind that only came once in a lifetime, if you were very lucky. Laurel knew now that no matter what, at least she had known that kind of love for someone. It was wrong not to tell him. It was an injustice to him—and to herself.

Feeling suddenly at peace with her decision, Laurel unknowingly fell asleep. She was awakened some-time later by a fierce banging on the front door that made her jump out of her skin.

She hurried to answer the door, her heart pounding as she fumbled to turn on some lights. Who in the world could it be? she wondered. Perhaps it was Jake Pratt, returning to check on her.

When she opened the door she was relieved to see Jake's familiar face, as she expected. But she immediately noticed his serious expression. And then she noticed the uniformed police officer standing beside him.

"Ms. Northrup," Jake began, "We didn't know how to reach you by phone…"

Suddenly the police officer stepped forward. "Mrs. Northrup, your husband has been in an accident at the airport—"

"An accident?" she echoed in disbelief. "But how could that be, he's in New York. He's not even—"

"He's at the hospital in Hyannis, ma'am," the officer cut in, calmly correcting her. "I'm sorry for the bad news, but we're sure there's no mistake. I think you'd better come with us right away."

Laurel tried to speak again but reeled from the shock. She felt her legs go rubbery and give way. Luckily, Jake stepped forward and caught her. The two men brought her inside and she quickly rallied. She had to go see Connor. He was hurt. Hurt badly, from the sound of it. She had to go to him. He needed her.

In the police car on the way over, Laurel listened to the details of Connor's accident and even asked questions, but it was hard to focus. Apparently, he'd discovered that she'd come up here and followed her in his plane, despite the bad weather. Something had gone wrong, just as the plane had hit the runway. They still didn't know for sure. The plane had touched ground nose down, then went out of control and skidded off the wet runway. It finally turned on its side, with one wing totally ripped off.

"They got him out quickly," the officer reported.

"But he's hurt and unconscious. His head hit the windshield, so he doesn't look very good," he warned her.

Laurel nodded and swallowed hard. She didn't give a damn what he looked like, she screamed inside. As long as he was going to be all right.

Laurel sat close by Connor's bed in the dimly lit room and held his hand, which lay motionless on top of the crisp white sheet. She'd been sitting in the same position for what seemed like hours. Watching and waiting for him to wake up. The police officer had been right, Connor looked bruised and battered, with bandages across his face and head, and injuries to his right arm and leg. He was listed in serious, but not critical, condition, the doctor had told Laurel. He had lost a great deal of blood and was weak. They'd given him some pain medication and most likely, he would not wake up until tomorrow.

Although the doctor urged her to go home and rest, Laurel politely insisted on staying the night, even if it meant sleeping sitting up in a hard plastic chair. She lovingly studied the rugged lines of his face, half hidden by the bandages. Then her gaze fell on the steady rise and fall of his chest and she sent up another thankful prayer that he had survived.

He still wore his wedding ring, she noticed, even though she had left her gold band and engagement ring in an envelope along with his note. She hoped it was a good sign that he hadn't removed his yet. Yes, it had to be a good sign, she thought as she leaned back in the chair and allowed her eyes to drift closed. It was a sign that there was hope for them yet.

"Laurel—" His voice was no more than a hoarse

whisper, but enough to rouse her from the depths of sleep. Laurel immediately sat bolt upright and leaned toward him. His eyes were barely open and she watched as he seemed to focus on her with great effort.

"I'm here. You don't have to talk now, sweetheart," she told him. Still holding his hand in one of her own, she sat on the edge of the bed next to him and touched his hair with her other hand. His eyes remained fixed on her face, wide and disbelieving, as if he thought he might be dreaming.

"I came back home, to tell you...but you were gone," he murmured bleakly, his speech blurred by the medication and the bandages across his jaw. "You didn't have to go," he added with effort, his expressive eyes underscoring his cryptic words with emotion.

Laurel leaned over him, cupping his cheek with her hand. "Maybe I shouldn't have run away. I think I've been running from you for months...maybe the past eight years," she added thoughtfully. "But I'm glad I came up here, Connor. I think I'm ready to stop running now. I was so afraid to tell you before, but I need to say it now—I love you. I have for a very long time. And I know I always will," she assured him.

"I love you, Laurel. Sometimes, I don't know how I managed to live all that time away from you. I was an idiot—and a coward—for not telling you how I really feel," he sighed. "I should have told you from the very start. That was the only reason I wanted to help you, and marry you. But I thought that the only way I could get you to agree was by making that horrible deal. I guess I was just too afraid of losing you, like the first time," he confessed. "Can you forgive me?"

"Of course I do," she said. But that was all she could say. She was overwhelmed with emotion. Her heart was overflowing with love and joy. "Can you forgive me for acting so horribly to you?" she asked hopefully.

"Of course I do…and I understand it all a lot better now. I finally found out what happened to my letter," he added. "Your brother, Phillip, found it."

"Phillip?" Laurel frowned. "But why didn't he give it to me?… And when did you hear that?"

"After I found out you'd left me, I called him, to see if he knew where you'd gone. Of course, he was delighted to hear that you had walked out on me. We had words and he brought up the past and actually bragged about how he'd kept you away from me the first time… But nothing's going to keep me away from you again," Connor promised her, gripping her hand with all his might.

Phillip. Of course. It all made sense now. So many odd comments he'd dropped during the years about Connor, as if he'd always known about their real relationship. But Laurel had never put it all together. How could she have guessed?

"It doesn't matter now," she promised him as she leaned closer. "As long as you're all right…and we're together again," she whispered tenderly against his lips. Then she paused to ask, "Do you think it's okay if I kiss you? I mean, will it hurt you?"

"I'm no doctor, but I'm sure I'll die of frustration if you *don't,*" he replied. And with his good arm, he pulled her closer so that her mouth finally met his in a deep, lingering kiss.

Before they had kissed for very long, Laurel suddenly picked up her head. Connor looked at her, a puzzled expression in his eyes. "What's the matter?" he asked.

"Nothing at all...but I have something else to tell you." She paused and took a deep breath. "I'm...expecting a baby. Our baby," she added.

"A baby?" Connor stirred, instinctively trying to sit up, but his movements were hampered by the tubes and wires attached to his body, not to mention his bandages. "Are you sure?" he asked eagerly.

Laurel nodded. "I'm a few months along."

"And everything's all right? You're not sick or anything?" He gingerly touched her stomach with his good hand, the look of awe and amazement on his face saying more than words ever could.

"No, not at all. Everything's quite normal," she assured him.

"Thank goodness. I'll have to take special care of you now. Both of you," he corrected. "God, I'm thrilled," he added.

"So am I," she said.

He gave a small smile and wound his arm around her waist again. "I thought you were getting sick from the stress of forcing yourself to stay married to me," he admitted. "That was the only reason I thought we should separate. I couldn't stand seeing you suffer just because I had to have you, any way I could."

"Shh," she hushed him. "Let's not talk anymore... I don't want to tire you out," she said sweetly.

"Good idea. No more talking," he agreed in a tired voice. Then she felt his hand at the back of her head, urging her closer for another kiss…an invitation she could not resist.

They remained that way for quite a while, kissing each other and murmuring loving words they had both longed to say and hear from each other. Finally, the heavy throat clearing of Connor's nurse caused Laurel to sit upright.

"Your blood-pressure monitor was going berserk out there, Mr. Northrup. I knew something was up," the nurse teased as she approached to check Connor.

"When do you think I'll get out of here, Nurse?" Connor asked eagerly while the nurse jotted down information on his chart.

"At this rate, you'll be out in no time," she answered wryly.

And that was good news to Laurel, who knew that her love for Connor and their children would fill her heart with joy and light through all the days to come.

Life with the man she had always adored had only just begun….

* * * * *

Silhouette Desire®

COMING NEXT MONTH

#1303 BACHELOR DOCTOR—Barbara Boswell
Man of the Month
He was brilliant, handsome—and couldn't keep his mind off nurse
Callie Sheely! No one had ever captured Dr. Trey Weldon's attention
like Callie, but she insisted their relationship would never work. Could
Trey convince Callie otherwise with a soul-stirring seduction…?

#1304 MIDNIGHT FANTASY—Ann Major
Body & Soul
Tag rescued Claire when she was in dire peril—and then showed her
the delights of true fantasy. Could this very real man of her dreams
save Claire from even greater danger—marriage to the wrong man?

#1305 WIFE FOR HIRE—Amy J. Fetzer
Wife, Inc.
What horse breeder Nash Rayburn needed was a temporary wife. What
he got was Hayley Albright, his former lover and soon-to-be doctor.
But Hayley still carried a torch for Nash. Could she rekindle *his* love—
this time permanently?

#1306 RIDE A WILD HEART—Peggy Moreland
Texas Grooms
Bronc rider Pete Dugan always knew that he was not cut out to be a
family man—then Carol Benson walked back into his life. Carol had
commitment written all over her, but when she revealed her long-held
secret, would Pete be ready to say "I do"?

#1307 BLOOD BROTHERS—Anne McAllister and Lucy Gordon
2-in-1 Original Stories
Double trouble! That's what you got when cousins Montana cowboy
Gabe McBride and British lord Randall Stanton traded places. What
Gabe and Randall got was the challenge of their lives—wooing the
women of their hearts. Because to win Claire McBride and Frederika
Crossman, these two blood brothers would need to exert all their
British pluck and cowboy try!

#1308 COWBOY FOR KEEPS—Kristi Gold
Single mom Dana Landry cared only about catering to the special
needs of her daughter. Then cowboy Will Baker taught Dana she had
to take care of *her* needs, as well—and he was just the man to help.
But when the night was over, would Will still want to be Dana's
cowboy for keeps?

CMN0600

If you enjoyed what you just read,
then we've got an offer you can't resist!

Take 2 bestselling love stories FREE!

Plus get a FREE surprise gift!